ENEMY DADDY NEXT DOOR

CALLIE STEVENS

1

———

AMY

THIS IS MY FAVORITE PART OF MY JOB, HANDS DOWN. Being able to read my books to groups of children nestled in the laps of their parents. After all, that's the point of writing a kids' book in the first place. Sure, I enjoy tailoring the stories and perfecting the art. But that all pales in comparison to being able to see children's faces lighting up with curiosity and excitement as they listen to the words leaping off the page and watch pictures coming to life.

That's what I'm doing today at the local library, the one I grew up going to just a short drive from my childhood home in Burbank. Who'd have thought that the little girl sitting on the reading rug with brown pigtails listening to stories would be the one telling them twenty years later?

Today is a book launch, which means I really have to sell it. It's the latest addition to my Petunia Porcupine series, my bread and butter. My publisher has made a buttload from selling these books. Finally, with this one, I really got to write what I wanted to.

"'Just because I'm not living here with you doesn't mean I won't think about you all the time'," I read aloud from the picture of Petunia's mother, Pansy, wiping a tear from her daughter's cheek. "'When I see a patch of wildflowers or feel a breeze come from the north, I'll think of you. And you know this isn't a goodbye. It's a…'"

I turn the page. An image of Petunia hugging her mother tightly (which is funny to think about since they're porcupines). "'…See you later.'"

I let the kids linger on the last page and then I close the book. "The end."

The kids applaud excitedly; the reactions from the parents are a bit more mixed. A few of them are bewildered that it ended on such a heavy note while others are truly gripped by the ending.

If they only knew how the first draft ended with Petunia never seeing her mother again. My editor, Fiona, said, "Don't you think that's a little *too* autobiographical?"

What's the point of being an artist if you can't work out your own trauma in your work? My mother left our family when I was still super young; unlike Petunia, I didn't see my mother again until ten years later when she pretended to want to reconnect with us. Talk about reopening the wound.

However, Fiona's assessment was fair. These *are* children's books. They might need to know about reality, but they don't need to know about how awful it can really be. I stuck to writing about Petunia's parents' divorce instead and gave it a bittersweet ending.

"Thank you so much for coming and hearing Amy Solace's newest book, *Petunia's Parental Predicament*," Fiona announces, swooping in front of me. "Did you all like it?"

There is a chorus of yeses from the kids although one of them cries out, "It was too sad." Their parents shush them.

I hold back a smile. Kids always speak their mind, regardless of if they should.

"It was sad, wasn't it?" Fiona says and glances back at me. "But I can assure you that Petunia has many adventures with both her mama and papa in the future."

The children celebrate.

"Now, for the parents, you have the unique opportunity of receiving a personally signed book from the author. Please, if you're interested, line up at the table of books. We take Venmo, cash, and card," Fiona continues, gesturing toward the back.

I take a deep breath and get to my feet. Alright. Show-time. Part two.

Despite the mixed response, most everyone has been dragged by their child to buy a signed book. I have a great time learning all their names and writing funny messages on the inside of the book covers.

"To Jemimah – I'll think of you when a duck quacks!" I write.

The little girl, Jemimah, grins, showing off her missing teeth. She pulls down on her shirt which has a big duck on it and laughs.

"Thanks for coming," I say, holding the book out to her father.

The man takes it and thanks me, but I can tell he was one of the parents who gave me a cooler reception.

I just have to remind myself you can be the sweetest peach in the world and some people don't like peaches.

Jemimah and her father walk off; the last person in the

line isn't a child, though. It's a grown woman accompanied by Fiona. I raise an eyebrow and smile.

"Amy, this is Gina Hendrix from the Burbank Chronicle. She wanted to ask you a couple questions about the book for –"

"The arts and culture section," Gina finishes and then shoves her hand so close to me it nearly knocks me in the nose. "Pleasure to meet you, Ms. Solace."

I lean back and take her hand. "You as well, Ms. Hendrix."

She shakes my hand with more strength than I know what to do with.

When I finally get control of my hand back, I drop it under the table and shake it out. That's going to leave a mark. "I'd be happy to answer your questions."

"Fantastic!"

Fiona pulls up a chair for Gina to sit across from me. She has a recorder to capture my answers and also writes at a breakneck speed on her pad of paper. She asks me all the usual things: why I'm a writer, how long I've been doing it, what I like best about it. Funnily enough, as a children's writer, people tend to ask me extremely infantile questions. I read interviews with some of my favorite fiction writers and am astonished at how cerebral the conversations are. But with me, interviewers ask me questions with the same cadence as if you were to ask someone what their favorite color was.

"Now this new book –" Gina picks up a copy from the table. "*Petunia's Parental Predicament.*"

"Yes."

"Interesting title. Tell us where it came from."

I smile, "Well, all of the titles in the Petunia series are

alliterative, staring with *Petunia, the Peculiar Porcupine,* which –"

"I've always found it so interesting you started your series with a title that seems to suggest that Petunia is a bit of a...weirdo, shall we say?"

I laugh. "Yes, that was the point! I wanted to create a character that was out there and so into being herself that people – or should I say porcupines – couldn't question it."

"A very 'be yourself' narrative."

Okay, this conversation is *fun.* "Precisely."

"*Precisely, Petunia.* That's actually one of my favorites. My kids love it."

"I didn't know you were a fan."

Gina beams. "Absolutely! I would have brought them if I wasn't on the job. And...well, that brings me to the subject matter."

My insides lock up. I knew I'd be getting backlash. It's one thing from parents who don't know what to do with themselves when their children's precious worlds are split with reality. It's another from a reporter for the Arts and Culture section. "Sure. Let's get into it."

"Literature about divorce for children is no longer uncommon as it once was. But it's interesting for you to introduce such dramatic subject matter into a series which many children read every volume of. Care to comment?"

I frown. "I don't know if I'd say it's a dramatic subject matter when fifty percent of marriages end in divorce."

Gina's eyes widen. "Well, divorce's impact on a child –"

"What I mean is, it shouldn't be so taboo to talk about. Don't your children have friends whose parents are divorced?" I ask. Then I clock Gina's ringless left hand. This is California – it's not uncommon for people to live in domestic partnerships even when children are involved. But from her reaction, I know I've struck a chord. "I was that friend. And because none of my friends were in that situation, they didn't know how to talk about it with me, because it was something no one could relate with. I felt like I was literally a weirdo, just like Petunia. But it was just a fact of my life. As simple as if you are right-handed or left-handed. Parents were either married or divorced."

"Well, forgive me, Ms. Solace, but that's usually a subject that parents prefer they seek out when the time comes rather than be shown it in a children's book series."

"That's just the thing, though. Children with happily married parents will read this and will be able to harness their empathy toward friends whose parents have chosen a life apart." I'm being much too generous to my own parents' divorce in this case, but I'm on the record. "I would have loved a book like this when I was a child. For me and for my friends who did what they could to be there for me, but just didn't have the capacity to understand it."

Gina's furrowed brow lightens. "I hadn't thought of it that way."

I shrug. "That's why you're a reporter, right? So you can ask the questions."

She grins. "I suppose you're right." She scrutinizes the book in her hands again and then says, "How much are these going for?"

"For you, Gina, it's on the house," I reply.

"Are you okay, Amy?"

I glance over at Fiona in the driver's seat. "Huh?"

"You've been awfully quiet."

I guess I have been. Since saying goodbye to Gina, I

haven't really said much. I've been caught up in my head. "Long day."

"Sure. I don't know how you do those readings."

"Just say the words on the page," I say with a chuckle.

"I couldn't do it. Reading aloud in front of people with the level of excitement and intensity you do. It's a skill. You should be proud."

I chew on my lower lip. I haven't ever thought about it like that. "Thanks."

"So, now that I've paid you with a compliment, what's really on your mind?"

I laugh. "Is that how this works?"

"It's like 'penny for your thoughts', but who needs pennies anymore?"

I lean my elbow on the arm rest, watching the street ahead of us unfurl as Fiona drives. "I didn't realize how difficult it would be to talk about my mom."

"I knew that's what this was about."

Then why'd you ask? "I still feel like I'm in a bit of a fog."

"I can tell. Not in a bad way, just –"

"No, it's good to know it's obvious. Means I still have some work to do."

Fiona is silent. The road rumbles beneath us. If she just dropped the subject, I'd be grateful. However, that's not the kind of friend she is. And I'm grateful for that too.

I guess.

"When's your next therapy session?"

"Tuesday."

"How's that been going?" she asks carefully.

I sigh. "Fine. That's always been fine. It's just...been a whole year since my mom came back and disappeared just as quick and...I'm still out of sorts about it."

Fiona smiles. "A year is not a lot of time, Amy."

I glance at my friend; she's about a decade older than me and has lived a lot more life. She moved away from home young, traveled the world, got married and divorced, cut off all her hair, became a masseuse and then dropped it all to edit children's books. That's a lot of life. Me? I've lived at home for almost twenty-five years, A.K.A. my whole life, and I write children's books. Sure, there's adventure within that, but not a lot of life experience. "You're right."

"You have to give yourself some grace. What your mother did to you was horrible."

I wince. Just because it's true doesn't mean it feels good to hear other people say it.

"And you're allowed to let it feel that way, but..." Fiona pulls the car up in front of my house and puts it in park. "That doesn't mean life on the whole has to be horrible too."

I smile. "That's good advice."

She rolls her eyes. "I don't know about that, but –"

"It is. Thanks, Fiona."

Fiona runs her hand through her bleached blonde pixie cut. "You're welcome."

I grab my purse. "Thanks for driving me today."

"Of course, any time." As I open the door and start to get out, Fiona calls out after me, "Remember we have a brainstorming meeting on Monday. Which means –"

"Yeah, yeah, come with my brain already stormed, I got it," I say with a wry smile. My publishers never actually want to be creative with me. They just want me to be creative and to pretend they are part of the process.

Fiona continues, "And then we have book signings on Wednesday and Friday, so –"

I shut the door behind me and shout, "I can't hear you!"

Fiona laughs and shakes her head.

I hold up my phone. "Just text me." Then, I turn around and head into the house, my smile immediately replaced with a labored sigh.

Life takes it out of me these days. Unless I'm majorly distracted with family things or aggravated by the next-door neighbor, I'm sluggish at best.

Doesn't help that my sleeping schedule comes and goes as it pleases.

Time to unwind, Amy. You earned it.

I drop my bag on the front stairs and head up to my room; I don't call out to let my dad know I'm home. He'll figure that out on his own. I just need a moment to myself.

It's a balmy July day and the afternoon sun is just starting to soften. Perfect time to go tan by the pool.

I slip on a bikini, grab my Kindle, and head down to the pool to sprawl out on a lounge chair and read the latest mystery by one of my favorite authors.

The second I settle in, though, I hear the sliding glass door of the kitchen open up and my dad call out. "Ames! Didn't know you were home!"

I put my Kindle down on my bare stomach and sigh. "Hi, Daddy."

My dad sidles up to the lounge and holds out a plate of strawberries and watermelon. "Snack?"

I can't stay annoyed for too long. He didn't know I wanted to be alone anyway. I slide my sunglasses up onto my head and take the plate with a meaningful smile. "Thanks."

"How'd the reading go?" my dad asks as he sits on the neighboring lounge chair.

I eat one of the strawberries, juicy and fresh beyond belief. At least I can still enjoy fresh fruit. "It was great. They loved it."

"I'm not surprised. It's a good one."

I glance at him carefully to see if he's lying. The first people who read my books other than my editor are my dad and four older sisters. I tried to keep *Petunia's Parental Predicament* from them until Kira swiped a copy of it from my room and read it herself. She then encouraged me to let the rest of them read it. I'm glad I did. "Thanks. I think it'll be mixed with reviewers at best, but –"

"Fuck 'em," Dad says, snatching a strawberry from the plate.

I laugh. Dad was always the picture-perfect parent when we were growing up. But once we matured and started having our own lives, he loosened up a bit. If there was ever a "cool dad", Kent Solace would be it.

"What are you doing with the rest of your day, baby-cakes?" he asks.

I gesture toward the pool. "This."

Dad grins. "Well, don't let me interrupt something important, then." He gets to his feet and tucks his hands in his pockets. "I was thinking we could do shawarma for dinner."

"Kira working late?" I ask. Kira and I are the only two who still live at home. The middlest and the youngest. She's got a high-powered tech job and, being one of the youngest people and the only woman on her team, she's always trying to prove herself. Plus, she hates shawarma. The only way Dad would ever suggest that is if she's not going to be home for dinner.

Dad sighs. "Yep. I wish she wouldn't work so hard, but..."

"Maybe I should be working that hard," I say with a half-laugh. "Staying up late into the night sketching or something." I've never been able to do the long-suffering artist thing. I like to work during the day, during regular working hours. Nighttime I can never get anything done.

"Are you kidding? You work your butt off. I'm so proud of you."

I can't help but get a little teary-eyed at that.

"Look at how far you've come. A famous author and artist, and you're not even twenty-five."

"I write kids' books, dad," I say. "That's hardly enough to qualify me as a 'famous author.'"

Dad narrows his eyes. "Don't sell yourself short, Amy. You're a famous author. Say it."

"I'm a..." The words make me want to gag. "...famous author." I break out into a full body shiver. "Ugh, that's so weird."

He grins and heads back inside, calling out over his shoulder, "Repeat that to yourself until you start believing it!"

I lean back in the lounge and stare out at the blue pool water. Yeah, I don't think I'm ever going to believe that one. Don't get me wrong, I'm grateful for my success. And I love what I do. I just always feel like a little bit of a fraud. That impostor syndrome always creeps in and says, "Not you. *You're* not worthy."

Relax, Amy. Time to let it all go and actually relax.

I finally settle in and let the California sun sink into my skin as I read. This is the life. At least it would be if I wasn't such an overthinker. California is not meant for over-thinkers. Everyone is so easygoing and freewheeling. Mean-while, here I am, my brain going a mile a minute and –

My "relaxation" is interrupted by a knock at the gate at the right of the yard. Our property abuts two others on either side. To the left is the Hitchins' and to the right is the Ricks' (if you can even call it that since they've only lived there for like a little over a year). Our fence has gates that lead into either yard. It's an old fence, so I've always chalked it up to people having more of a sense of community back in the day. You could just open your gate and waltz over into the yard to visit a neighbor.

Now, though, we rarely use them.

So, the pummeling knock at the gate makes me jump out of my skin until I remember who lives next door. *Hunter Fucking Ricks.*

"Is anyone out there?" a female voice squeaks, trying to temper its volume.

My blood runs cold. *You've got to be fucking kidding me.* I get to my feet and pad around the pool deck toward the gate. To the surprise of no one, when I open it, there's a woman standing on the other side. A California-model type. She wears an urgent expression on her face but that doesn't make up for the fact she is barely wearing anything on her body. She's got her bra on and a skirt, but her top (however skimpy it might be) and her shoes are dangling in her hand.

"Can I help you?" I ask.

"Thank goodness you answered," she says, smiling and tucking a lock of hair behind her ear. "Hunter told me I could come through this way, and I already called my Uber, so I didn't want to –"

"Well, for future reference, you can't," I say coldly. My yard is not an escape route for Hunter's lady du jour.

The model type's eyes widen. "Um. Alright." She sneaks her foot through the gate and slides past me. "Won't happen again. But thank you." Then, she breaks into a run down the side of my house and out through the gate to catch her car.

I tighten my hands at my sides and stare at the open gate. This isn't the first time this has happened. But it will be the last if I have anything to do with it. Maybe my anger is a bit out of control. After all, it's just a gate.

It's more than just a gate, though. It's an invasion of my family's privacy, a disgusting display of what kind of man Hunter Ricks is, and just another reason why I hate the man.

I storm through the gate into the Ricks' family yard. Today is the last straw.

2

———

HUNTER

I LEAN AGAINST THE KITCHEN COUNTER AND WATCH the coffee start to drip into the Chemex. I need a pick me up after the session I just had with Therese. Or was it Terry? Doesn't matter. I probably won't see her again.

I run my hands through my hair, still wet from the shower, and adjust my towel around my waist, just in case Jessica wakes up and comes downstairs from her nap.

Look, just because I'm having little trysts at home while my daughter sleeps doesn't make me a bad guy. We all have needs. And I'm a busy man. All the free time I have, I dedicate to Jess. So, I have to squeeze in things for myself where I can.

It's called self-care.

Before my coffee finishes, much to my chagrin, the front door opens. "Fuck," I say to myself. It better not be... Tabitha? I really got to get better with names. I told her explicitly to sneak out the back and go through the gate into the Solaces' yard to avoid being seen in case Jessica woke up or was awake and looked out her window. If she left something behind, she should know better than to just storm in here and...

"Hunter!"

That's not Trisha's(?) voice. That's the voice of a seriously pissed off Amy Solace. What the hell is she doing storming into my house without an invitation?

"In here," I call out. I might be confused about what she thinks she's doing, but I have to admit, I'm curious.

"I need to talk to you." I can feel her anger without even seeing her face. Which is funny because when she walks into the kitchen and lays eyes on me, her entire face goes red and her jaw drops. "Oh my god! What are you doing?!"

My coffee's done, so I pour the delicious bean juice into a mug. "Having a cup of coffee. What are *you* doing?"

Amy holds out her hands and gestures toward my lower half. "Not – not the coffee! You're –" Her embarrassment gets the better of her and she flips away from me covering her face. "Oh my god!"

I laugh to myself. "What are you so embarrassed about?"

"You're – you're naked!"

"I'm not naked. I'm half-naked." I take a sip of coffee. Perfect. Bold and strong. Just the way I like it. "There's a difference."

"I won't talk to you until you're clothed."

Now it's my turn to clock what she's wearing. Tiny bikini that's barely covering her ass. I'm ashamed to admit I've taken some long looks at her out by the pool since Jessica and I moved in a year and a half ago. It's even better up close. However, I'd never want to make her uncomfortable with my gaze. I'm her much older neighbor. Her dad would kill me. I look away. "I could say the same of you."

Amy looks over her shoulder at me, her silken brown

curls cascading down her back. She crosses her arms over her chest and huffs. "You've got some nerve."

"I'm just saying I think we're even," I reply. "Now..." I take a few steps toward her. "What is it you wanted to talk to me about?"

Amy's body softens when she remembers her purpose in coming here. "I've had just about enough of your girl-friends sneaking through my yard."

I resist smiling. So, that's what this is about, huh? "They're not my girlfriends."

Her body locks up again and she ducks away from me toward the other side of the kitchen island. "You know what I mean."

"I don't think *you* even know what you mean, Amy. These are women I have fun with. Nothing more," I explain.

Amy gapes at me and then darts her gaze away again. She can't bear to look at me for more than a few seconds at a time. Surely, it can't be for my *propriety*. I'm a grown ass man. Perhaps Amy is concerned about *hers*. What year is this?

"You feel inclined to have fun with them in the middle of the day and then send them out through a stranger's yard in broad daylight?"

I lower my voice and follow Amy's trajectory around the island. "I can't have them going through the house toward the end of Jessica's nap. Plus, her window looks out at the front of the house. She'd see them walking out front. Best to keep things completely separate."

Amy looks outright disgusted with me as she backs away. It's sort of cute. Sort of.

"Have you considered that maybe it's not appropriate to

have women traipsing through your home with your daughter upstairs?" she says in a tense whisper.

"Have you ever considered I am a man with needs?" I echo back in the same tone. I love teasing her. She gets so up in arms about it.

She makes a noise of frustration and turns away again.

I laugh. "You may as well turn around; clothes aren't going to magically appear on my body."

She does so, begrudgingly, her eyes very purposefully focused on my face rather than my body. Which I have to say is a feat. Not that I think much of my body, but I do keep it in good condition. It shouldn't surprise her that I've got a line of suitors. "If it falls off and you flash me, I'll sue."

"Trust me, Amy, this is on as tight as a chastity belt."

Her eyes widen briefly. And though I'm still a few feet away from her, I'm evidently too close. She backs up and hits the kitchen counter,

"See?" I jump up and down. The towel doesn't move. "I'm a pro at this point."

"Can you not do that? You're making me uncomfortable."

I stop. Never in my wildest dreams did I want to make her uncomfortable. There's a line between teasing and discomfort, and I'm embarrassed to have crossed it. However...it didn't take much to get Amy flustered. Perhaps she lacks the experience I've just assumed she had. Not for any other reason than she's a beautiful young woman, surely sought after by suitors.

If she's withheld her virginity this long, major kudos to her. I know men can be fucking pushy. I clear my throat and take a step back. "I'm sorry. That wasn't my intention."

Amy's eyes flick down briefly to my chest and maybe even farther down, toward my waist. Her cheeks flush.

Then, she looks away. "I won't be an accomplice to your behavior again."

Listen to her talking like we're in a courtroom or something. "What's that mean?" I ask with half a smile.

Amy glowers at me. Really, she glares, her deep brown eyes smoldering like she wants to kill me. Too bad it just...stirs something inside me instead.

Down, boy. Next door neighbors are off-limits. Girls nearly half your age are definitely *off-limits.*

"It means that the next time one of your little playboy bunnies knocks on the gate, I'm not letting them through. She can do the walk of shame on *your* property." She turns on her heel and starts to walk back toward the foyer.

Don't look at her ass, don't look at her ass. "Come on, Amy. It's not that serious," I say as I follow her into the front hall, keeping my voice low in case it travels up to the second floor where I know Jessica is probably starting to stir from her nap.

Amy shoots back around; her eyes aren't just smoldering now, they're full of fire. "*Not that serious?!*"

"Okay, keep your voice down, Jessica is just upstairs," I say, trying to temper her anger.

Her hands ball up in front of her and her lips tighten together. "You are the most infuriating man I've ever met."

Why does that feel like a compliment?

"Amy, I'm sorry I upset you, but don't be unreasonable, alright? We're neighbors."

"Neighbors are for a cup of sugar! Not exit strategies for pl—"

"Playboy bunnies. Got it."

Amy lifts her chin. "Now, if you'll excuse me, I'm going to go enjoy *my* family's pool on *my* property, *uninterrupted.*"

"By all means," I say, gesturing toward the door.

And, with a final flounce of her luxurious brown curls, Amy stomps out the door.

"Don't slam the –" I cry out after her, but it's too late. The door cracks loudly as it shuts behind her. Great. Now Jessica is *definitely* awake.

I sigh heavily. Well, that's a way to interrupt that post-coital flow. Back to reality.

I climb the stairs and head to my room where I throw on a casual linen shirt and khakis before going to check on Jessica. I softly crack the door, praying that she's deeply asleep and couldn't possibly have heard any of that conversation.

To my chagrin, she's sitting in a beanie bag in the corner of the room turning the pages of a book. But not just any book. *Amy's* latest book.

Just my luck that my nemesis next door neighbor is my daughter's favorite children's book author.

"Whatcha reading, Jess?"

My little girl lifts her eyes over the top of the book and squeaks. "*Petunia's Parental Predicament.*"

Shit. Not again. Ever since I got the advanced reader's copy of this book from Amy, Jessica has asked me to read it to her nearly every night. The girl loves books more than anything, but ever since this one arrived, she's barely been interested in a trip to the library or the bookstore.

And even though she still can't read books on her own completely, she remembers them. I've found her reading along with me, saying the lines that Amy has written. It's like she's obsessed with it. And the last thing I need is for my little girl to be obsessed with a book about divorce.

"Woof. *Petunia's Parental Predicament,* huh? That's heavy."

Jessica snickers. "Are you a doggie, Daddy?"

"Woof, woof, woof," I bark and drop to my hands and knees. I crawl over next to Jessica and snuggle up beside her.

She giggles and rests her little head on my shoulder. "Will you read it to me?"

"Uh, you sure? Haven't you read this a bunch of times by now?"

"It's my favorite."

Amy's not only her favorite writer, but now this is her favorite book? I'm doomed. "Maybe another time, kiddo. You know how I feel about stories like this."

Jessica closes the book and puts it down on her lap. It's so big it basically obscures her legs completely. "You don't like stories about sad mommies and daddies."

I try to be honest with her. I know what it's like to be withheld from emotionally. That was my entire childhood and then some. It's my main goal in life to make sure Jessica feels loved and safe. Especially when it's just me taking care of it. If I have to sustain my romantic life with one-off flings, so be it. Jessica needs all my love. "I don't, sweet pea," I say, softly brushing her dark hair from her forehead. "I'm sorry."

"When won't mommies and daddies make you sad?" she asks with a frown. A genuine question. In fact, a good question.

"I don't know, honey. You know, Daddy's been through a lot."

Jessica touches my hand, running her fingers along the veins that have started popping out as I've gotten older. "Maybe if Mommy came home, you'd feel better."

Oh, fuck. Sometimes this kid just says things and stabs me right in the heart. Jessica doesn't have memories of her mother, unless she has some memory that started freakishly early. "You know I've told you, Jess, Mommy can't come home."

Jessica's shoulders fall as if she's hearing that again for the first time even though I've said it *so* many times. In fact, she's been bringing it up more and more as she's gotten older. My excuses are lame and limp. Unless I tell her I don't want to talk about it, I don't think she'll stop asking. But that doesn't feel fair. I don't want her to become an adult and have all this built-up resentment toward me because I shut her down from asking about things she deserves to be curious about. "Mommy loves you. That's why she's not here. I know that's confusing."

Jessica sucks in her cheeks. "Okay, Daddy."

She buries her head in the crook of her arm and takes long steadied breaths. I can tell she's trying not to cry. Where do they learn this? When do they start holding back like this? Is it my fault she's not having tantrums and kicking and screaming because she wants something she can't have?

I kiss the top of her head and rub her back. "Hey, what do you say to going out for some ice cream?"

Jessica lifts her head and smiles despite the sadness at the corners of her hazel eyes. A perfect combination of her mother and me dancing together in her irises. That's what life was supposed to be like. Like the color of my daughter's eyes. "Will they have chocolate?"

"Are you kidding? I bet they'll have double chocolate chunk! Come on!" I scoop her up off the beanie bag, reveling in her excited scream.

At least I can still distract her with ice cream. But it's only a matter of time before that trick stops working too.

3

———

AMY

"You want to do a follow-up to divorce?" Fiona asks with a sour face.

I have to laugh. "You sound absolutely disgusted, Fiona."

Fiona gapes and then looks to the rest of my team. "That's not what I meant."

I grin. "I know that."

"It's just...a heavy follow up to a heavy book in the children's market feels a bit like –"

"A risk?" I ask, glancing at the storyboard I made last night that now sits on an easel in front of my agent, editor, and a couple interns.

My agent, Kris, picks up where Fiona left off. "What I think Fiona means, Amy..." Kris is from Oxford and talks like she thinks she's better than you. She terrified me when I had my first meeting with her. However, now that I've been working with her for several years, I know it's completely out of her control and she's actually a sweetheart. "...is that we've done the divorce thing and we need to move on."

Most of the time. "It's no good to just tell kids that

divorce happens and not follow up with a comprehensive guide for them to handle it. It's an ongoing grief. Something that will always be a part of them. It's going to affect them their entire lives. All of their relationships. It's..." I scan the room. *Okay, Amy, you're going a tad overboard...* "It's traumatic."

"We know, kitty," Kris says. "The book has also been traumatic, to put it lightly."

"What do you mean?" I ask with a frown.

"The book on divorce was a risk. But we did it. because you, Amy, are a star. It's a simple point of fact that Petunia is quite nearly a household name in terms of children's literature."

Must be a pretty small group.

"But..." Kris says, pursing her lips and looking down her nose at me through her cat-eye glasses. "The reception has been mixed. It vacillates between triumphant and vitriolic in both reviews and the messages we are getting from readers."

I sigh. "So, what does that mean?"

"I hate to rein you in, kitty, but..." Kris looks back to Fiona. A handoff of sorts. They'd make a good pair on a football field.

Fiona takes a deep breath and looks me in the eye. "This next book can't be heavy, Amy. No follow-up to the divorce."

"No death," Kris says pointedly.

"No violence," Fiona adds.

"God, no."

I look at the storyboard, my heart sagging in my chest. *Sorry, I did my best.* The story had already started coming alive inside me. Petunia being shuffled between her mom and dad's houses, not knowing how to keep track of her own

life. I never dealt with this, but...it's the best I can do with
the market.

At least I thought it was.

"So, back to the drawing board, kitty!" Kris says.

I hate it when she calls me "kitty".

"We want something upbeat! Something positive.
Something that has some quotes we can slap on a motiva-
tional poster and teachers can put in their classrooms."

"Oh, that's a great idea!" Fiona cries out. "You have
some of those, don't you, Amy?"

I don't write books to put quotes on fucking posters. I
write them because I want them to mean something. I want
to help children understand how they feel. I want more kids
not to have to walk around with the ache I have to carry
with me at all times.

I force a smile and nod, "Absolutely."

***

I LOOK OUT THE WINDOW. Thank god I had therapy right
after that shit show of a pitch meeting. The yellow and red
striped couch is super uncomfortable, but not more uncomfortable than my therapist's stare when I don't know the
next thing to say.

I sigh. "Um, I don't know. Just want to write what I
want to write, I guess." Jordan and I have already gone over
the whole debacle at the office and worked through the feelings there. Now it's just about biding time until we're done.

"You're holding something back, Amy."

I look at Jordan with alarm in my eyes. "What?"

She smiles. "We've been working together for a lot of
years, Amy. I can kind of tell."

It's true. I met Jordan when I was eighteen after my

child therapist broke up with me (to be fair, I just aged out of child therapy, but still). Jordan was newly married. Now I'm a writer and Jordan's a mom. I feel close to her even though we aren't allowed to be friends or hang out outside of therapy. "I hate when you do that," I say with a smile.

"I know, I'm sorry."

"No, don't be sorry, I..." I laugh. "You're just right. And sometimes, I hate when you're right."

Jordan shrugs and turns to a new page on her legal pad. "So, what's on your mind?"

I screw my forehead together and realize what's buried underneath everything is something I simply don't want to talk about. But if I can't talk about it with my therapist, who can I talk with about it? "It's about my neighbor."

"Is he still bugging you?" Jordan asks.

It's embarrassing how many times I've talked about Hunter in our meetings. I just can't help it. He keeps grinding my gears. From blasting music in the middle of the day while I'm trying to draw in the yard to his cavalier attitude about his personal life, the man drives me mad.

This last infraction, though...I can't seem to shake it. My heart beats with anxiety when I think about that woman coming through our gate. "He just...one of his conquests snuck out through our backyard. And I was out by the pool, so I had to, like, *deal* with her. I mean, she barely had a shirt on."

"Hmm. That's strange."

"Right? It was so uncomfortable. Turns out he *sent* her out that way. Which is just so presumptive that he thinks he can just send people through *our* yard so that his daughter doesn't see."

"Why do you think it's making you so upset?"

I haven't even said as much, but she must be able to tell

by the way my voice is going shrill as I give her more details. "I...I don't know. But every time I think about it, it just makes me furious. *Furious.*"

"Jealous, maybe?"

I scoff. "Jealous?! No."

Jordan laughs. "Okay, just asking. I know you've mentioned he's handsome before and, well, wanted to make sure we weren't dealing with a crush situation."

I stare at Jordan. A *crush*? On *Hunter Ricks*?!!! That might as well be a death wish. "That would never happen."

"Okay, I get it. He's not a nice guy."

"No, it's not that he's not a nice guy. He's at the very least a good dad. You know, a single father."

"That takes a lot of work."

I nod. "I know that. Of course I know that." I remember how frazzled Dad was when Mom left. Being eaten alive by five girls. At least he had Dana, but still. "He's a fine guy. Just not to me."

"Has he been outwardly rude to you?"

Rude to me? "No, I guess not."

"But..."

"There's an unspoken rivalry."

Jordan chuckles and writes something down, "Oh, *is* there?"

"What are you writing down?"

"Nothing."

"You just wrote something down."

"Yeah, that's what I do, Amy. I take notes on you," Jordan says.

I twist my lips to the side. "I hate when you do that."

"You wouldn't like to hear what I wrote down."

My eyes bug out and I lean forward. "Why are you

telling me that?! Now you're just making me want to know what the heck you wrote down!"

Jordan smiles. "Look, these notes are just for me. They're not facts. They're not things I believe. They're just thoughts that come up...as they come up. So, if you really want to hear it, you can't let it get in your head."

"This seems like bad practice from a therapist," I say with narrowed eyes.

"Well, with other clients, maybe. But we've known each other six years. There's a little bit more leeway."

I think very hard if I want to know what she's written down. Can I bear walking out of this meeting and not knowing the observation Jordan is making about me on the privacy of her paper? "Fine. Tell me."

Jordan pauses for a considerably long time.

"Jordan!"

"Alright, alright. I'll come out with it. I'm wondering if this anger is misplaced. Maybe it's covering up for a different feeling."

I look at her incredulously. "What kind of feeling?"

"I don't know. Something more to do with *liking* Hunter, maybe?"

The way she says "liking" sounds suspiciously like the way we used to say "like-like" on the playground when someone had a crush. "You don't mean to say you think I have *feelings* for that man, do you?"

"Now, I told you not to jump to conclusions about what I've written," Jordan tries to temper my shock.

"No way! There's no way..." An image of Hunter standing before me without a shirt on and that measly towel covering his...God, I feel hot around the collar just thinking about it and I've never even had that part of a man anywhere near me. "Okay, maybe not no way, but..."

"Ah..."

"Jordan!"

She smiles like she's eaten the last cookie from the jar. "Sorry."

"It's just...if I feel anything. Which is attraction, at most. Physical attraction. Certainly not mental given his propensity to –"

"Ooh, good word."

"Thank you, I'm a writer."

We both giggle.

"Anyway, he's not my type. And it would never in one million years happen."

"Why?"

"Jordan!"

"Amy! What?!"

I grunt in frustration. "You're not helping."

"I'm sorry, I'm just trying to get you to look at the thing you've been ignoring. Won't that feel better than just glossing past it for the one millionth time?"

Yes. I know it will. We spent our first two months of sessions with me glossing over my mother. Eventually, I broke down. It feels so much easier to ignore a problem until it's been buried so deep down it erupts like a volcano, spewing smoke, ash, and lava all over your life.

But have I really been doing that with Hunter?

"Even if I did feel that way, which I'm not saying I do –"

"Of course," Jordan affirms.

"He's much too old for me."

Jordan tilts her head from side to side. I can tell she's about to refute this idea. After all, my older sister is married to a man over twenty years her senior and everything seems to be hunky-dory.

"And he doesn't actually care about any of these women. He's just looking for a piece of ass to pass the time."

"Well, then that's a good reason to stay away."

I chew on the inside of my cheek. Even if I were a different kind of woman, a woman who felt free enough with her body to give it to any man she pleased, Hunter wouldn't be interested. All the women who traipse through his life are the bombshell bimbo type.

Well, that's not fair to those women. Just because they look a certain way doesn't mean they don't have worthwhile careers or intelligent thoughts. But most of them have that bleached blonde hair, fake boob lifestyle that permeates Southern California.

That's not me. I keep my hair natural, I'm kind of short in comparison to the model types, and definitely don't dress like them. I'm much more inclined to a pretty floral dress than something so tight to my skin it looks impossible to take off. God, even thinking about it makes me claustrophobic.

"He wouldn't ever be interested," I say to Jordan definitively. "Not that I'd even want him to be."

"Of course," Jordan replies. She clicks her pen and strikes through her note. Why does that simple motion of her pen tear through my heart? Sure, I just said it's an impossibility, but now that she's indicated that, I want to prove her wrong. "I'm glad we followed the thread."

I nod. "Me too."

Although, the truth is, I just started following this thread. And from the looks of it, it's going to take a lot of time to unwind.

4

HUNTER

How about nine?

I LOOK AT MY PHONE UNDER THE CONFERENCE TABLE.
It's from a number that I've only marked as Blonde Kelly.
Although all the Kellys I've ever known have been
blonde.

I type out a quick response while keeping my eyes
focused on the board member who is droning on and on
about the Ricks Group's latest project.

Make it ten. Give my daughter time to get
to sleep.

The message immediately gets a heart react and then
the three dots appear to indicate Blonde Kelly is typing.

I turn off the screen and focus on the conversation
again.

"I don't think our shareholders are going to be too keen
on the Ricks Group focusing in on becoming a competitor
to Disney."

"We're not," I say sternly. "We're just expanding our

market. We've gotten luxury hotels down to a science. The family friendly sector is incredibly lucrative."

"And unstable," the elderly board member mutters, crossing his arms over his chest. "And I'm sorry, but I have a hard time thinking you're taking any of this serious with that hair of yours."

I laugh despite myself. My hair is tied tidily back with a ponytail holder. Perish the thought of how he'd react if my hair was hanging down past my shoulders as I have it everywhere else in my life. "Stan, my hair has nothing to do with this. You're grasping at straws at this point."

"Well, I think your parents would be rolling in their graves if..." Stan starts to drone.

I immediately tune him out. Any mention of my parents makes my brain shut off. I need to retreat away so as to not think about them. Thankfully, my phone buzzes right at that moment. I let my eyes glaze over as I listen to Stan, pretending to listen long enough that he won't be offended I look away. Then, when it's finally time, I glance down at my phone.

Blonde Kelly. Thank god.

Okay, I'll be there. Can't wait. Already thinking about what I'll do to you... ;)

A message like that usually makes my body flush from stem to stern, makes my imagination run wild thinking about all the possibilities for my encounter with Blonde Kelly.

This time, though, I feel nothing.

Oh god. There's no way I'm old enough that I need some sort of Viagra or something, right? Besides, I was fine just this weekend. No way that all just turned off at once.

I swallow.

I know why.

It's because I have someone else on my mind. Someone who marched into my kitchen with her bikini on and enough anger to mow down an army of men.

Amy Solace.

I'm ashamed to admit I have a little crush. She's so much younger than me. And she totally hates my guts. What kind of person am I to be attracted to a woman who can't seem to stand me?

"Hunter!"

My attention snaps back to Stan.

"Are you listening?" the older man sneers.

I lean back in my chair and smile casually. "No, I wasn't."

Some of the other board members have to resist laughter.

"The disrespect, young man – "

At least at forty-two I'm young in some people's eyes. I glance at my watch and then push myself up from my seat and sigh. "We're moving forward with the project, Stan. There's no ifs, ands, or buts. Now if you'll excuse me, I've got another meeting."

I don't wait for any replies from the peanut gallery. This is my company. What I say goes.

I just can't believe this is what I turned into after resisting it for so long.

My meeting is only one in name. I'm meeting up with a couple friends for midafternoon drinks which means the rest of my workday will be worthless.

That's just fine with me.

When I arrive, my friends are already there. Axel and Grant are sitting at a high-top right by a set of doors that opens up onto a back patio so we can get the perfect combination of air conditioning and LA heat at once.

The three of us have become a sort of unlikely group of friends. Mostly because we all came together through the central force of the Solace family. Axel's childhood home is on the other side of the Solace property, so we would run into each other often. Grant, of course, is Kent Solace's best friend and ended up falling in love with one of his daughters. It was only a matter of time before the three of us gathered together and realized just how alike we are.

"You're late, Hunter," Grant says with a wry smile.

"Sorry, was trapped in a meeting."

"They're still giving you a hard time about the project?" Axel asks. Axel is a property developer; we met as neighbors, but I enlisted him to help me with finding and developing the family friendly resort I want to add to the Ricks Group.

I hold out my hand to flag down the server and simultaneously murmur, "It's not a hard time if they know they don't actually have much of a say." When the server stops by, I order a whisky sour, then return to my conversation. "I'm just waiting for them to shut up. We're moving forward with it as soon as you find the right spot to build."

"Well, you're in luck, I actually –'"

"Did I really come all the way out here for you two to talk about work?" Grant asks, rolling his eyes.

I can't blame Grant for being annoyed. He's got a not-so-newborn at home and is doing his best to run a multi-billion dollar entertainment company while also being a supportive husband and father. "You're right, sorry. You gotta tell us how married life is," I say.

"The same as unmarried life," Grant says. "Harley and I only wanted to have the paperwork done. Makes more sense, especially now that Tana is here."

Grant and Harley had a courthouse wedding and the reception of the century just over a month ago. "Well, what about you?" I turn to Axel. "How does it feel to be a 'fiancé'?"

Axel flushes. He's usually a stiff upper lip kind of guy, but any time he starts to talk or even think about Gillian, he gets bashful. "I have to say it *does* feel different."

"*That* I'll agree with," Grant says.

I felt different at every step of the way with my ex-wife. Boyfriend to fiancé to husband all felt like mounting accomplishments.

Ex-husband and single father really just popped all that like a balloon.

"I have to admit, though," Axel says, twisting the base of his gin and tonic. "With Stella in the mix, I have moments I get really nervous."

Grant and I exchange a look. It was different for both of us. We both had time to prepare for fatherhood and were with our daughters every step of the way. Axel just found out that Gillian's daughter, Stella, is his. And Stella is six. "I see you two together," I say kindly. "You make it look easy."

"I don't know many men who could step up like you have, Axel," Grant adds with a nod.

"I just don't want to become my dad," Axel says carefully.

We all go silent. We've all expressed that sentiment at one time or another. That's really the thing that binds us all together: we're fathers who are desperate to break the patterns of our own childhoods. "You won't," Grant says.

"You say that so confidently," Axel replies.

"Because I have to!" Grant exclaims and picks up his martini. "Because I think that every morning when I wake up."

"We have to believe that we won't in order to make it through, I think," I say.

The server comes by, dropping off my drink, and I down half of it in one go. The number of times I have laid in bed awake at night thinking about how I'm not enough for Jessica. How I will never be able to fill the shoes of both a mother and a father because inside I'm so broken and twisted around...

I have to wake up and believe that being a father is a job I'm meant for. Everyday.

The absence of Jessica's mother notwithstanding, I think I do an okay job most of the time.

"I don't know how *you* do it, Hunter," Axel says. "I mean, I say that to Gillian all the time. How you do it on your own. You deserve a fucking medal or something."

"If you were in my shoes, you would have stepped up too," I say.

"Don't sell yourself short, Hunter," Grant says. "Take the compliment."

More than a friendship, Grant, Axel, and I have formed a support group. I didn't know how badly I needed it until we stumbled into a heavy conversation at a party in the Solace backyard that simultaneously made me want to crawl out of my skin and also alleviate the pressure of keeping my feelings bottled inside for the past...I don't even know how many years.

It's our version of therapy.

"Just because there were unhappy parts of our childhoods doesn't mean that we don't know what a happy one looks like. I think that's something we just take for granted from a traumatic childhood. I mean, look at the Solace girls. They went through all that with Aileen, and I haven't heard Harley question once her ability to be a mother to Tana," Grant explains.

That's true. "Chalk that up to Kent, I guess," I say.

"Yeah, talk about a man who stepped up," Axel adds.

Grant smiles to himself. That *is* his best friend. "Maybe we could all take a couple pages from his book."

I've been trying to take pages from Kent's book. However, I've never had the confidence to ask him outright for his advice. I know the pain I feel over being a single father. I can't imagine how it feels from his perspective, left with five daughters all over the age of ten. With Veronica, my ex, I always resent how she didn't try. But Kent has to look at his ex-wife and realize that she tried and then opted out.

I don't know what's more heartbreaking.

"What do you think, boys? Some apps?" Grant asks, opening up the menu.

"Please, I'm starving," Axel says.

While they pour over the options, I retreat back into my thoughts. I'm more like Kent Solace than either of these guys, at least in the parenting sphere. I am fathering on my own.

So, why the hell does Amy hate me so much? Shouldn't she understand where I'm coming from? Did Kent Solace *really* never need to unwind and treat himself? I mean, he had five daughters running around, for Christ's sake! I can't imagine the pressure and stress. That man *deserves* a break every now and then.

Maybe that's the problem. Maybe Kent Solace is the model single dad and I'll never live up to that potential.

However, if Amy thinks I'm some sort of bad dad to Jessica, I think that would just about kill me.

Grant and Axel start arguing over the different dishes. I'm about to cut in and make an executive decision (leave it to three businessmen to not being able to resist arguing over something as simple as appetizers) when my phone buzzes.

Another text from Blonde Kelly. I open it.

> What can I bring tonight? Champagne? A
> friend?

I sigh. This girl has just suggested a menage a trois and I'm not the least bit excited. I think I need a break.

I text back quickly.

> Something came up. Rain check.

Then I turn off my phone and put it away, leaving the thought of Blonde Kelly behind me.

If only Amy Solace could see what a good guy I was being. Perhaps then I could get on her good side.

5

———

AMY

"Okay, I've mapped out the house into sectors," Kira announces, putting her notebook out on Gillian's coffee table. "I've assigned everyone certain sections with time allotments. If we buckle down, I think we can have all of this done by six."

Dana, my eldest sister, beams. "Wow, Kira. You did an amazing job with this."

"Yeah, seriously, you're a lifesaver," Gillian adds while distributing glasses of champagne to all of us, each of them garnished with a strawberry.

Harley and I remain silent, giving each other a look. *Classic Kira.* As the two youngest, we both know how this is going to go down. We're going to get started, people aren't going to be focusing, we're going to get trapped in looking at Stella's baby book or wondering why Gillian has so many rolls of wrapping paper and then Kira's going to be furious when at six we don't even have a fraction of what she wanted done.

We were *born* into the Solace systems and habits. They weren't made around us. We were fit into them as best as our parents and sisters could. So, that gives us an amazing ability to see the forest for the trees.

"And we're drinking why?" I ask as I take my champagne glass.

"Because this is a celebration!" Gillian grins. "It's not every day I pack up my house in order to move in with my fiancé."

"And baby daddy," Harley adds.

"Exactly, this is big for me," Gillian replies, settling into the couch next to Dana.

Dana wraps her arm around Gillian and kisses the top of her head. "My baby is growing up!"

We all laugh. "Plus, it helps Stella is out with Dad and doesn't have to see us day drinking," Gillian says, swigging her champagne.

"Okay, well, then this deserves a toast," I say, getting to my feet.

"Shouldn't Gillian make the toast?" Harley asks.

"I'm the youngest, so I get to make the toast," I retort.

Harley rolls her eyes. "Oh, I *forgot*. You're the *youngest...*"

My sisters giggle while I glare. I hate being reminded that I'm one of the prime examples of youngest child syndrome. I can't help that I was the smallest for so long and want to be the center of attention when we get together. My sisters all make up for it with their own versions of crazy, that's for sure. "To Gillian's next step of her wild journey."

"Hey!" Gillian interrupts.

"Wild is an affectionate word in this context," I explain. "You've worked tooth and nail to make your bakery dreams come to life, all the while with Stella right by your side. I don't know of anyone more deserving of this happiness and love you're cultivating with Axel."

Gillian smiles at me. "Oh, Amy...you always know what to say."

"It's because she's a writer," Harley says with a sly smile.

I scan my sisters' faces. Each of them is so unique and special. I don't feel that way. Sure, I *am* a writer. It's a unique sort of job. But sometimes it's hard to see the beauty in yourself that you see in other people. Dana cultivates friendships like flowers, Kira works her tail off in tech despite all the adversity she faces as a woman, Harley is curious and full of spitfire.

What am I? A good girl?

I guess.

"To Gillian," I say with finality, unable to look at the saccharine side of life any longer or else I might just combust into an existential crisis.

"To Gillian!" all my sisters echo.

We hurriedly clink glasses, gabbing as we sip our champagne.

"Well, let's talk about boys, shall we?" Harley asks with a smile.

My mind immediately goes to Hunter, and I try to erase the thought away as hard as I can with an eraser that doesn't seem to be doing anything but making the picture murkier. I hope no one can see on my face the excruciating pain I'm in thinking about this man I can never have, nor do I really want.

Harley turns to Dana. "So, how are things with –"

"Don't even think about it," Dana interrupts, holding up her hand.

Harley looks at me with wide eyes. "Oh my god."

"Did something happen?" Gillian asks excitedly.

"No, nothing has happened. Nothing will *ever* happen,

and I've told you this literally one million times because Drew and I are – "

"*Just friends*," the rest of us finish her sentence.

Harley shakes her head. "Lame. When are you guys going to realize there's something there?"

Dana used to be Drew's grief counselor. Since he left her practice, they became fast friends. In fact, he's always her plus one to any Solace family gathering. And yet, after all these months, nay, years of friendship, nothing romantic has happened. At least that's what she's *saying*.

"You two would be so cute together," I say dreamily.

"You're living in a dreamworld, Amy," Dana says.

That hurts a little bit. Nicks the outside of my heart. I might be twenty-four, but they all still treat me like a baby. When are they going to see that I'm just as grown as they are? Maybe with less life experience, in lots of ways, but I deserve to be taken seriously.

"Enough about me. I want to talk about your birthday, Amy."

"Oh god, that," I say touching my forehead.

"Don't you dare react that way!" Gillian exclaims. "You're turning twenty-five! That's nothing."

And yet, it's a quarter of a century in my mind. "I know, but..." I'm a virgin who still lives at home with my dad. I cannot express to any of my sisters how deeply embarrassing that feels.

"What do you want to do, Ames?" Kira asks, turning her analytical, bespectacled gaze toward me.

"I don't know. I just want...I just want it to be quintessentially Solace," I say with a smile. "You know, something for us as a family. I don't need anything fancy or a paint and sip like last year or...Something at home would be nice."

Harley claps her hands. "That's easy, then. A cookout."

"How does that sound to you, Amy?" Dana asks me carefully.

I nod. "That sounds perfect."

An alarm goes off. Kira launches her hand into her pocket and pulls out her phone. "Okay, chatting time is done. We have to get started on round one of packing if we're going to get out of here at a reasonable time."

"You set an alarm?!" Harley asks incredulously.

Kira downs her champagne and stands up. "I've set several alarms. You'll be hearing them throughout the day. Okay, now, Dana and I are going to take the kitchen while Gillian gets started in Stella's room. Harley and Amy, I want you to focus in on the closets."

All of us stare at Kira, the master planner.

She claps her hands. "Chop chop!"

Dana and Gillian jump to attention and start to titter about, gathering moving boxes and packing material.

Harley lets out a heavy sigh and then grumbles just loud enough so I can hear, "I should have just stayed home with Tana. That would have been more relaxing than this."

I laugh heartily and give her my hand. "Come on, we'll make it fun."

"THIS IS...WORSE THAN I THOUGHT."

Harley and I are staring into Gillian's hall closet that is packed to the brim with...everything one could possibly imagine. It's clear this has served as both a pantry for dry goods and just a place to chuck things she didn't know what to do with. There are cans upon cans of beans piled up next to a picnic basket and a bag of rice on the ground that's starting to spill out onto a couple boxes of boardgames.

"Do you think she'd notice if we just threw all this out?" Harley whispers.

"I heard that!" Gillian shouts from Stella's room across the hall.

I look back at Harley. "There's your answer."

My older sister groans and then collapses on the ground next to an empty box. "Okay. Let's get started."

I've let Harley be the packer while I do all the heavy lifting. It's clear from the bags under her eyes that the exhaustion of motherhood is still ever present as it was when Tana was fresh out of the womb. So she sits while I sift. Just fine with me. It lets my mind focus on other things like, why does Gillian have so many cans of hearts of palm that have expired, rather than worrying about my impending twenty-fifth birthday. "Okay, maybe we should just start with sorting things."

"Sounds good to me."

I start handing Harley can after can.

"I liked your new book, Ames," Harley says.

I smile. Harley was notably missing from the family read of the newest addition in the *Petunia* series. I didn't hold it against her. I saw Gillian as a new mom. I know as well as I can what a haze it can become. "Thanks for reading it."

"Of course! I went straight to the bookstore on launch day and bought my copy. I've read it to Tana a couple times, but I'm not sure she understands yet."

I laugh. "Of course she doesn't."

"Truthfully, it made me tear up. It was really beautiful."

I sigh, handing her a can of coconut cream. "Yeah, I'm proud of it."

"Must have been hard to write."

"Honestly, not really. What's harder is that my

publisher doesn't want to hear any more stories like that for now."

Harley's eyes bug out. "What?! That's crazy."

I shrug. "They're saying it's too sad."

"Well, fuck them."

"Harley!"

"Don't tell me you haven't thought it!"

I flush. "Okay, fine, yes, I have. A little."

Harley and I exchange a smile.

"Anyway," I say, getting to my knees and shuffling around for any other errant cans. "How are things with Tana?"

Harley takes a deep breath. "Great. I'm exhausted, but you know, I wouldn't have it any other way."

Harley really has taken to motherhood in a way I never anticipated.

"I mean, it helps Grant has just been amazing. He's a great dad and really does his best not to make me feel like I'm doing all the labor."

"No pun intended."

"Right..." Harley pauses thoughtfully. "The only thing is he's already starting to talk about when we're going to have another one. And I'm just not ready."

I stop sorting through the closet and drop onto my bottom beside Harley. "He's not pressuring you, is he?"

"No, no, not at all," she says earnestly. "Grant's just worried about getting older. He wants to be around as long as possible, so..." Harley bites back on her words.

I hate that while my sister is confiding in me about her husband's concerns about aging, my mind is once again drifting to Hunter Ricks. "It must be difficult with the age difference," I say softly.

Harley laughs sadly. "To be honest, I don't even think about it most of the time."

"Really?" I gape. It's all I'm able to focus on with Hunter.

Then again, I'm not in love with him.

"Really. Grant and I are best friends," she says.

"Don't let Dad hear you say that."

Harley rolls her eyes. "It's different. We just get each other. The only times I realize how old he is are when we talk about having more children and when he complains about his cholesterol."

I laugh loudly.

"What?! It's true!"

"I know, I just didn't even think about that."

We both remain silent for a few moments with our backs up against the wall. Feels like we're little again, sitting outside Dana's room while she and Gillian talk about Mom and Dad in hushed whispers, not wanting us to hear because we were "too young".

"I think about how he's going to start changing faster and faster as the years go on. But so will I. And so will Tana," Harley continues. "But who he is won't really change. Our connection won't change. I hate to say it, but age really is just a number when you have a connection like we do."

My heart is pumping hard in my chest. "That's beautiful, Harley." More than that, it's made me excited. Between my conversations with Jordan and now Harley, Hunter Ricks doesn't seem like such an untouchable entity anymore.

He's just a man. A very handsome man with long black hair and more muscles than I knew existed who is starting to sneak into my subconscious more than I'd like him to...

Still. Even if I open my heart to him, it just feels like I'm setting myself up for failure. He'll never see me like I see him. I'd just be dooming myself to a crush that will make it impossible for me to be around him.

"Don't worry about us, Amy," Harley says. "Grant and I are fine."

I don't have the heart to tell my sister it's not her I'm worried about. It's me.

I MANAGE to sneak out around eight. Yes, we obviously ran way over Kira's precious schedule much to her chagrin. Gillian's house is topsy turvy, boxes and things scattered everywhere.

And don't even get me started on the tension. Everyone is ready to snarl at each other the second something goes awry. That's one of the downsides of having so many sisters. When we get angry, we get *feral*.

But first, we're passive aggressive.

When I said I was leaving, Kira looked at me with lasers coming from her eyes. I thought she might just melt the lenses of her glasses with that look. "What do you mean, you're going?"

"I mean that I need to get home. I've got stuff to do in the morning for work."

"We all have stuff to do for work, Amy," Gillian retorted.

"I have a meeting first thing in the morning!" I replied.

Dana gave me a doe-eyed look. "Amy, we all promised that we would help Gillian get things ready to move in with Axel."

"I know that, but it wasn't supposed to –" I'm the

youngest. I can wiggle my way out of most anything. I used to be able to do it by being cute. Now I'm twenty-four and no one falls for that anymore.

Kira cut me off before I could finish. "You know what? Go. We'll be fine."

It was very clear that it was *not* fine. Still though, with four sisters, I operate under the assumption that if people aren't saying they're mad at me, I couldn't possibly know that they are. So, I smiled and said, "Great!" and left without another word.

I try to release all that pent up tension on the drive home, deeply sighing over and over. I roll down the windows, feel the California air tickle my skin. But it's no use. No matter how much sighing I do, I can't shake Hunter from my brain.

I'm starting to get embarrassed of myself. And the only person who knows is me! I'd probably die if anyone else got wind of my teensy crush.

When I get home, I trudge into the house. No one else is home. Kira is back at Gillian's, obviously, and Dad is still out with Stella. That means I can just...unwind. I go up to my room, ready to immediately collapse onto the bed and wallow in my building dread.

I drop my purse, flick on the light, see the beautiful haven of my bed waiting for me...

But I stop as I pass by my window and notice Hunter down in his yard.

He's sitting at the edge of his pool, legs dangling in the water. His long hair looks freshly brushed, cascading over his shoulders. And he's reading. He's reading a stack of children's books. I can't help but stare, watching him as he turns page after page, illuminated by the moonlight.

Suddenly, he turns to look up at me.

Shit, he must have noticed I was watching. Felt my eyes on him or something.

I freeze like a deer in the headlights. It'd be childish to duck away and hide behind the curtains although I wish I could. Pretend this never happened at all.

Hunter's face cracks with a smile. He raises his hand and waves at me.

I raise mine slightly to wave back. *God, I feel so stupid.*

Then he pulls his hand toward him a few times. I'm confused at first until I notice it's a "come hither" sort of wave.

"Come down," it looks like he mouths.

I swallow. This is a bad idea. I should just shake my head and smile.

However, how can I relax knowing I've left this man hanging? Knowing he...wanted to see me?

I take a deep breath. I might regret this.

But it's time to start living.

6

HUNTER

I don't know what compelled me to invite Amy to sit down here with me. It was an impulsive, gut feeling. My body said screw it before my mind could catch up, and suddenly, I was waving her down, asking her to come here to sit with me.

I guess I just couldn't help it. It felt cosmic. Me sitting down here reading her books. Then her appearing at her window. The vision of her illuminated with her long brown curls tumbling over her shoulder and her brown eyes watching me with tender curiosity...

It's a divine sight.

I'm a grown fucking man, though. Many years her senior. I should be able to rein it in, control myself.

I just can't keep from thinking about her.

To my delight, Amy nods and holds up her finger, mouthing, "One minute," and then disappears from the window.

I try to busy myself with reading, but I can't seem to calm my nerves. The words on the page jumble together and my heart leaps into my mouth. *Fuck, this is going to be creepy, isn't it? A grown man reading her books? She'll think I'm some kind of freak.*

When the handle of the gate jostles, I sit up straight, alert and waiting.

Amy emerges from behind the door with an amused smile. "You don't lock the gate from your side, do you?"

I laugh; easier than thinking of something to say at the moment. "I didn't know it locked at all."

"You've got a lot to learn about this place, then," Amy says teasingly.

I blink. Is she...flirting with me? Where is that girl trembling in my kitchen at the sight of me in a towel just the other day?

"Some light reading, huh?" Amy nods toward the stack of books as she comes to sit down at the pool's edge.

I watch as she crosses her legs, her airy pants pooling around her like water. "You might recognize them."

She screws her eyes together for a moment. Then they pop open wide. "Oh! You're reading *my* books."

"I am," I say with a nervous chuckle.

"Definitely some light reading, then!"

I shake my head. "No, not at all. I mean, compared to Tolstoy or Faulkner, but..." I close the book in my hands and look at the cover. *Petunia's Patience Problem.* A classic. "You know, Jessica loves these. I've read them to her countless times. But I've never really stopped to think about what you were actually saying."

"Hate to break it to you, Hunter, but there's not a lot of symbolism hiding in my work. At least not compared to Tolstoy or Faulkner." Her lips perk up at the end. A sad kind of smile.

"You shouldn't undersell your work, Amy. You're a talent. I've got a stack of books here that proves that."

She flushes and rolls her eyes bashfully. "Well, thank you. That's nice of you to say."

"It's not nice. It's true." My eyes meet hers briefly. Anything more I could say flies out of my head. Her beautiful eyes just take my breath away. This is so wrong. Even the girls I keep on rotation aren't as young as she is. *She's just a girl, Hunter.* "Your new one in particular is pretty..."

"Heavy," she says, staring out at the pool. The pool lights illuminate the ripples on her face.

"You say that like it's a bad thing."

Amy sighs. "Because it is."

I furrow my brow. Unsure what she means.

"It took a lot to get my editors to agree to even letting me write the book. Now they won't let me forget what a big risk it was and how it's causing a lot of readers to be up in arms."

"That's ridiculous."

"Right?!" she asks, snapping back toward me. "She might be a porcupine, but the point is that she deals with real problems."

I chuckle. "I see what you did there..."

Amy raises an eyebrow.

"The point? She's a porcupine..." I trail off.

Amy bursts out laughing. "That wasn't purposeful *at all.*"

"Sorry. I'm a dad, I think in puns."

"Trust me, I'm familiar with that."

Great, so now she's thinking of me like she thinks of her dad. It's for the best but way more disappointing than I'd like it to be. "Well, from one of your fans, I'm really glad you wrote this book."

Amy smiles. "You don't know what that means to me, Hunter. Thank you."

I become very aware of my legs dangling in the pool,

floating back and forth. There's a chill now in the air and it's starting to make me shiver. "I wish I'd had something like this when I was a kid."

"That's exactly what I said!" Amy then hesitates. "Were your parents divorced?"

I laugh dryly. "No, but they should have been."

"Oh, I'm sorry."

I shake my head. "Don't be. It's my life. I have to face it. No use being sorry about it. Besides, they're dead, so."

Amy gasps. "God, I'm sorry I brought it up."

I wave my hands. "No, no. I didn't mean it in a sad way. It's just a fact." I'm sort of surprised she doesn't know. Their death was national news. I guess maybe she was too young to care. Just another reason why I shouldn't be having thoughts about her. I was in my mid-twenties while she was roaming the playground. "I'm just saying, like...it's good to make kids face what's real. Especially if it will help them cope with something. This one has quickly become one of Jessica's favorites, so thank you."

"I'm glad she likes it."

"It's made her ask me a lot more questions about her mom, which I don't necessarily know how to answer, but... it's better than her pushing it all down. I know what that's like. And it isn't a good thing."

Amy nods. "Yeah, I can't imagine how challenging it must be for her to understand when she's so young. I was thirteen and I can still barely wrap my mind around it."

I study Amy for a moment. Whenever I've seen her, she's either bubbly or in the midst of a tirade. I knew this part of her must exist. After all, she's a thoughtful writer. But I thought maybe she just saved it for the pages. Now, though, a different side of Amy is cracking through. "Parents are...tricky," I say. *Understatement of the century.*

"Yes, they are. I'm lucky my dad is the way he is, though. I can't imagine how hard it's been for him."

"Your dad is..." I shake my head. "If I can be half the dad he is, then I'll have done a good job."

"He is a pretty good dad," Amy says. "And so are you. From what I can tell."

I want to immediately refute that. But I don't. Take the compliments where I can. "Thank you. It doesn't always feel like that." I swallow. I don't talk about this stuff openly. Well, actually, I do now. With Grant and Axel. I used to keep it close to my chest. The funny thing about vulnerability is once you do it a little bit, you want to do it more and more. It's like a drug. "My dad was nothing like Kent Solace type."

"Oh yeah? What type was he?"

"A 'never around' type," I say, raising my eyebrows. "You know, running a hotel conglomerate takes a lot of work. And his generation was so much about work...not about family at all. So, we were so disconnected. And he didn't know how to care for me at all. Never said 'I love you' or 'I'm proud of you'..." I trail off. "And you know what, I don't think it was because he didn't know how to say it. I think it's because he didn't feel it."

"Hunter, don't say that," Amy admonishes. "That's not fair to you. Of course he loved you. You run his company!"

I bite back a bitter laugh. If only she knew the stories about that. "I want to be better. I never want Jessica to question how I feel as her father."

"I'm sure she doesn't. You're so good with her."

"You say that, but –"

"Hey! I mean it!" Amy retorts. She grabs my arm and squeezes it. "I mean it."

Why did she have to touch me? Just the way her hand

wraps around my bicep sends shockwaves through me. I close my eyes, try to stave off the attraction stumbling through me, but I can't. It's too quick. Too unavoidable. *Deep breath, focus.* "Thank you."

"You're welcome," she says.

The second her hand drops from my arm, I want to grab it and put it against me again. I restrain myself. "I'm sorry I invited you down here to just burden you with all my problems."

"They're a nice distraction from mine," she says jovially.

"That's good, I guess," I chuckle.

Amy and I smile at each other; she looks away first, her smile fading, eyes drooping at the corners. I continue to watch her, willing her eyes back to mine. Something is happening here. Something I haven't felt in years. *Years.* I feel my body charged around women I want to sleep with, no question. But this feeling is deeper. My heart is opening to her. And that terrifies me.

"Can I tell you something you can't tell anyone?" she asks, her voice soft and wavering.

"A secret? For me? To what do I owe the honor?" I smile crookedly.

Amy shakes her head. "I don't know. Maybe just hearing you talk about your dad or...I'm not sure, but I feel like I have to say it."

My mind runs through a never-ending list of possibilities of things she could say.

"Sometimes I text my mom."

Oh shit.

"She never replies."

It's not my life, not my mother. And it still feels like a slap to the face. "Amy, I'm so sorry. That must be so hard."

She raises her eyes to mine. They're glistening with unshed tears. "It is. It really is."

I remember last year when Aileen came back after leaving her family ten years prior. Rearing her ugly head back into the lives of the girls she abandoned for her own selfish desires. Every time I saw Kent, he looked like a terrified chihuahua. A storm cloud seemed to linger over their house. Then, when Aileen left again, the clouds parted, revealing the beautiful blue California sky.

It's foolish to assume the storm cloud didn't leave any damage in its wake.

"I don't know what's wrong with me. Why she couldn't possibly want to – to know me." Amy shakes her head. "That thing you said about your father never loving you or never being proud of you. I don't think I've ever put words to that feeling until just now."

I can't watch her fall to pieces like this. Amy is so kind and sweet. So full of goodness. How could her mother ignore that?

Amy begins to cry. She covers her face, shaking her head. "I'm sorry, I didn't mean to –"

I slide closer to her and touch her shoulder. "There's no need to apologize."

"I just...god, why am I crying?" she asks, the judgment of herself clear in her voice.

"Because you needed to cry. That's alright." Until Jessica, tears to me were abhorrent. Mostly because tearfulness was not allowed when I was a child. In my quest to give Jessica the love and life I did not have, I have welcomed her tears. Every one of her emotions is welcomed in our home. Consequently, I feel the same about the people around me. Just because I'm a businessman who sleeps around doesn't mean I can't see the true range of people's emotions.

I rub Amy's shoulder, my thumb digging into her bare shoulder. I want to be closer. I want to pull her into my arms and…

It's wrong. Especially when she's crying.

But I can't ignore electricity.

"Do you want a hug?" I ask. It comes out more awkward than I'd like it to.

Thankfully, Amy nods with vehemence and collapses toward me. I don't have time to question how to position my arms. I just wrap her up in a tight embrace and whisper, "It's okay. You cry it out."

She buries her face in my arm and weeps. God, the top of her head is right there. Her beautiful swirls of caramel hair…I'd love to press my nose into it and breathe in deeply.

I rub her upper back. "You're okay, Amy. I promise, you are okay."

Amy's sobs abate and she lifts her head. The rims of her eyes are red, lips swollen, cheeks glistening with tears.

So fucking beautiful.

"Thank you," she whispers. She's so close I can feel her words tickling my chin. "I needed that."

"Of course. I…" I can't take it anymore. That gut impulse is back, the one that invited her down to sit with me out of my control. That was innocent.

This impulse, though, is much worse.

Because this one is pushing me to kiss her.

So, I do.

7
<hr>

AMY

Hunter Ricks is kissing me.

I repeat, *Hunter Ricks is kissing me?!* I can hardly believe it or comprehend how this has happened. One second, I'm sobbing in his arms (how embarrassing) and the next, his lips are pressed against mine in the most wonderful kiss I've ever had.

It's hard to describe what makes it so wonderful. Perhaps it's the way his arms are wrapped around me, not willing to let me go. Or the way he tilts his head minutely in order to make me feel the depth of his passion.

Or maybe it's just because I wanted this *so goddamn bad.*

Hearing him open up to me stirred my insides more than I can describe. I had Hunter all wrong. He isn't just a sex-starved man who has the maturity of a frat boy. He's complicated. Has pain he's trying to undo. It made me like him so much more.

In fact, it made me want him.

As his lips continue to caress mine, I slide my hands

around his back, cupping his shoulder blades. I swear, he moans when I touch him. I feel the vibrations in my lips.

I don't have a lot of experience in this department. But Hunter does and I can tell. He finesses his tongue into my mouth with both gentleness and insistence. I can feel his want just through his kiss.

Not to mention how one of his hands cups the back of my head while the other slides lower and lower down my back until he's dangerously close to my backside. A part of me is terrified that he can sense my inexperience and it will somehow turn him off, disgust him from being entangled with me like this. The other part of me wants *more, more, more*.

"Touch me," I whisper raggedly against his lips, grabbing tightly to the collar of his T-shirt. "*Please*."

And as if he can read my mind, that hand that has strayed lower and lower now grips at my ass, pulling me close to him, almost into his lap. The pool water sloshes as he pulls his legs out of the pool so there are no boundaries between us. The water seeps into my clothes, but I don't care. I don't care what kind of mess we make.

He kisses me. Hard. Ferocious. But not painful. I can feel his need reverberating through his body and into mine, like we're syncing together more than before. I slide my hand down his chest lower and lower, feeling his rock hard abs. What would happen if I reached under the hem of his shirt and felt them for real?

What has gotten into me? Would I let him if he asked? Even if I never have...?

Sex shouldn't be as mystical and far off as it feels, but it is. I've never had the confidence to just "get it over with" as so many women I know have done. I want it to mean something. I'm not waiting for marriage or anything like that, but

I want it to be with someone who will cherish the moment just as much as I will.

I can't believe I'm considering that Hunter might be that man.

The kiss ebbs, much to my chagrin. Hunter's fingers trail against my temple, tucking some hair behind my ear. "Amy, your lips are..."

"What? What's wrong with them?"

He chuckles, wide, gleaming smile. "Nothing wrong. They...they taste so good." Hunter has a deep voice, and yet somehow it's deeper than it's ever been. Rumbling in his belly like a tumbler polishing rocks into gemstones.

I throw myself back into the kiss so hard, Hunter gets knocked back to the ground, absorbing my energy into his chest. His beard hair rubs at my skin, and I relish the rawness.

"Amy —" he says breathlessly, but I don't give him a chance to finish.

I'm insatiable. All of the moments Hunter has annoyed me have built up to this. Maybe Jordan was right. A part of this frustration might have been sexual.

Hunter pulls his lips from mine and tucks them up against my earlobe. I feel the slight brush of warm saliva. "Not here..."

Oh, god. He's talking about...sex. This is all moving a little too fast for me. Okay, a lot too fast. But now I'm here in his arms, his hands dangerously close to creeping under my dress to feel my bare thighs and ass and I can feel a sneaking, telltale swell in his crotch, pressed against my pelvis.

"Let me take you..." He drags his lips from my ear to my neck and begins to kiss it nourishingly. "Somewhere more..."

Vibration. Between us. Not metaphorical. Literal. He stops speaking when he feels it.

Bzz-bzz…bzz-bzz.

It stops. I resituate myself on his chest and frown at him.

Hunter catches his breath, eyes glued in mine. His expression is…guilty.

Bzz-bzz.

"What's that?"

Bzz-bzz.

"My phone," he answers. "I just have to –" His hand moves toward his hip.

I recoil from my place on his chest, returning to sit up at the pool's edge. "Oh, right, yeah. Sure."

Nothing to spoil a moment like a phone buzzing. Or maybe more than that, nothing spoils a moment like a man who feels compelled to *check* his phone. Am I not entertaining him enough? Would he rather be anywhere else but here?

I watch Hunter's brow furrow as he looks at the texts on his phone. "Give me a minute," he says softly and then gets to his feet.

"Where are you going?" I ask before he can get more than a few steps away. If he leaves now I might lose my nerve before he returns.

Hunter hesitates and runs a hand through his long hair. "There's someone out front, I just need to let them know now isn't a good time…"

It hits me all at once. "Oh my god."

"It'll be quick, I promise. No more than two minutes," he says, trying to back away.

"Oh my god!" I cry out and jump to my feet. "Is this one

of your girlfriends? Did you have a hook up scheduled for tonight?"

Hunter inhales tightly. "Again, I don't have 'girlfriends', Amy."

The moon overhead feels like a spotlight shining on me. Not in a good way. "You know, don't bother telling her to go," I say softly. "I don't want to get in the way of your plans."

"Amy, I don't want you to go."

That tugs at my heartstrings. I *want* Hunter to want me. But not like this. Not when this emptiness could have been filled by one of those playboy bunnies. "No, I'm not just another one of your girls. I don't want you to think I'm a part of your rotation or something."

Hunter is quiet at first and then he laughs in disbelief. "Amy, I had no idea that you were going to come over tonight and we were going to..." He gestures toward the poolside, unable to find the words.

I remember how much older he is than me. He looks it right now in the moonlight, shadows casting heavier in the wrinkles in his forehead. This makes everything feel even worse. He should know better than to use a young woman like this, just to fulfill some sort of primal need. He has a daughter for Christ's sake. How is he going to teach her to value herself if her own father has girls on tap in every area code? "You could have told me you were busy. You shouldn't have even invited me down," I say, my jaw tightening so my words come out clipped and stern.

Hunter's eyebrows jump. "Now wait a second –"

"You can't be alone for one second? You always need some girl f-fawning over you?" I feel all that rage I felt at the girl running through our yard return to me. That kind of anger that emboldens me in ways I still don't seem to be able to understand enough to rein in.

"You can't be seriously angry at me about this, Amy."

My anger flares. "Of course, I can!"

"We just had a really nice conversation about some really intense stuff and that wouldn't have happened if I hadn't invited you down here, alright? How was I supposed to know that it would lead to anything more than just being friendly? How was I supposed to know that you'd kiss –"

"*You* kissed *me*," I interrupt. "Let's get that straight."

Hunter turns his head slightly. "You're right. That's true."

"So don't *blame* me for –"

"I'm not blaming anyone! That implies there's something to be blamed for and I don't see any of this as being –"

"I do. Because it was a mistake."

Hunter opens his mouth to speak but stops. He tucks his tongue into the side of his mouth, his cheek bowing outward and he looks down.

I can't say it felt like a mistake. But given what I know now, how could it be anything but? He was just...biding his time with me. It wasn't anything to do with feeling for me or enjoying my company. All I am is a way to pass the time to him.

I can't believe I even considered giving my body over to him.

"If that's how you feel, I'm not going to convince you otherwise," he says coldly.

And just like that, we're strangers standing in the moonlight as if we haven't just twined our bodies together. As if I just haven't told him something I haven't told *anyone* else. Why did I feel so compelled to trust him? Something in those caramel-colored eyes. Tempted me. To taste and trust.

A sweet, delicious treat. Turned out to be a sticky trap instead.

"*I* enjoyed your company," Hunter adds in earnest. "However you feel about it is your own prerogative."

He enjoyed my company. And it can't have been only for the physical. That wasn't implicit. We sat here and talked for god knows how long. He had to have enjoyed that too to have "enjoyed my company".

Just as I'm about to respond, his phone buzzes loudly in his hand again, the screen lighting his face, tainting the moon-filled night. Any impulse toward forgiving and forgetting disappears in an instant. Hunter's hand clenches around the phone, lips in a tight line. "I have to –"

"Yes, you two have fun," I murmur and turn on my heels toward the gate back to my yard. "Don't let me stop you."

I don't know what I would have done if Hunter called out after me. Tried to stop me. Because he doesn't. He picks the easy way out. The thing that's familiar and doesn't require work.

Not me.

I slam the gate door behind me and lock it; the bolt scraping with disdain. That should be enough to let him know that his little plaything is not welcome to leave through our gate.

There's a light now on in the kitchen. *Fuck, Dad's home.* He's probably going to want to hear about my day, ask me how packing went, ask me where I've been. I couldn't possibly deal with an inquisition right now, not with how my eyes are pricking with tears.

I tuck myself up against the fence and sink down onto my bottom, pulling my legs up to my chest. My cheeks still burn from embarrassment.

I let Hunter Ricks in for a split second, and he's managed to somehow break my heart. So utterly. How is this possible?

The worst part is, I knew better. I knew he was too old for me and that his flippancy toward sex and intimacy would somehow break my little heart.

Yet, I let it happen. I let it happen because for just an instant, I wanted something that didn't make sense to want. I hoped. I risked. I did all of those things they say you have to do for love...or something like it.

And I failed spectacularly in less than half an hour.

What is *wrong* with me?

I'm going to need to contact Jordan for an emergency session. That much is obvious.

8

―――――

HUNTER

I lean my chin in my hand as I watch Jessica pick up a whole pancake with her fork and try to eat it. I've taught her how to cut things into bite-sized pieces, but she is adamant it's faster just to stick things onto the fork and do her best.

Makes for a show with every meal, I'll tell you that. However, her hair has gotten quite long and I'm slightly terrified she's going to end up with a wad of maple syrup in her hair.

No matter, my mind is elsewhere. Half of it is on my steaming cup of coffee and how badly I already need a second one.

The other is on Amy.

In fact, my mind has been on Amy from the second she left a week ago, when we were interrupted by those awful text messages. To say I felt like an idiot would be an understatement. I couldn't have known that Amy and I would find our way toward each other like that. If I had known that, I wouldn't have invited her down. Or, I wouldn't have even considered inviting a woman over for the night. The first I had invited since Amy came to my house in that damned bikini.

Amy felt like a second choice. And Amy Solace should *never* feel like someone's second choice.

She wasn't mine. She was my first that night and she continues to be my first whenever my mind gravitates toward the thought of being intimate with someone else or even just...just talking. In fact, that woman had been second choice to her. A means to an end. A way to see if I could take her out of my head.

Because for that whole time, I want it to be Amy.

"Want a bite, Daddy?" Jessica asks, holding her fork out with the half-eaten pancake.

I smile through my tiredness. "No thanks, honey."

Her eyes look at me emphatically. "You look hungry."

Not for food. Not hungry at all for food. For an opportunity. However, I indulge her spirit and take a nibble of her syrup soaked pancake. "Mmm, sweet," I say, my mouth bristling at the saturation of maple. "Not as sweet as you, though."

Jessica grins and shakes her head, putting the pancake back into a pool of syrup. "So silly, Daddy."

Having a kid makes being a person hard. They notice everything. They can sense changes in mood and the way that you're reacting to them. But they're too small to understand it and certainly not nearly mature enough or old enough to be a sounding board for your issues. I'd obviously never ask that of Jessica. First of all, she's three and, second of all, it's important to me that she stay carefree for as long as possible.

I remember being a very serious child at home. At school, I was a class clown and would act out, which made for lots of visits to the headmaster's office. At home, I had to be good. Especially around my father. He saw me so infrequently that when he *was* home, he expected me to be an ornament in his life, not an actual child.

That's the opposite of how it should be. I want Jessica to feel as free as possible to be her whole self when she's at home with me. She should feel safe to act out and feel her emotions, knowing I will always be here and love her, even if we have to work through some complicated things.

My smartwatch buzzes on my wrist. It's an alarm to let me know it's time to get Jessica in the car for day camp. That's something that helps me a lot as a parent. *Alarms.* Alarms for bedtime, alarms for school drop off and pickup, alarms for dinnertime. When you're a single parent, a truly "I'm-on-my-own" single parent, sometimes you need to make your alarms your copilot. "Okay, Jess, last few bites. Then we have to brush our teeth and jump into the car for camp."

Jessica takes a humongous bite, tearing a majority of the pancake off her fork. She leaps out of the chair and puts her fists on her hips. "Ready!" she shouts with a mouthful of pancake.

I laugh and grab a wetted paper towel to wipe the stickiness off her mouth. "Explorers don't explore with syrup on their face."

"You're right. A wild animal could sniff me out from a hundred miles away," she replies with a serious expression. Then, she pulls her tiny neon green binoculars to her eyes and stares up at me. "Whoa, you look weird through these."

I pick her up off the ground and throw her over my shoulder. I know sending her up to brush her teeth will be a fruitless task. She'll get distracted looking at everything in the house through those tiny binoculars. Jessica laughs and hammers her fists on my back. It's more like a wimpy massage than a fight. "Put me down, scallywag!"

I chuckle to myself. The camp I have her enrolled in was at the recommendation of Gillian Solace. In fact, many things are at the recommendation of Gillian. I have a parent crush on her, which means I just admire everything she's been able to do with Stella as a single mom. I've gone to her many times with questions, concerns, looking for recommendations.

The "Wild Explorers" camp has definitely been one of the best so far. Jessica comes home every day with wild stories of nature hikes and animal spottings. Best of all, she's zonked by eight most of the time.

I drop Jessica in front of the mirror. She steps onto her little stool to see herself in the mirror, grabs the child-sized toothbrush, and holds it out in front of me. Fulfilling my part of the routine, I grab the bubblegum-flavored toothpaste and drop a splotch of it onto her brush.

With the toothbrush sticking out of her mouth, she points out the door. "Get the Jeep ready!"

"Yes, ma'am," I reply and head back downstairs.

I don't drive a Jeep; I drive a Hummer. But she's really into all this explorer stuff. Maybe I should look at making a switch...

I head outside toward the car, which is bulbously parked in the front driveway. But I slow down as soon as I hear a familiar voice.

"...I'll be fine, Dad."

Amy's voice. Sweet and bubbly as ever. Not the way it was the last time I saw her.

I duck out of sight behind the car.

"It's a long drive. Just call me when you get there," I hear Kent reply.

I peek out from around the car and watch as Amy springs toward Kent's Jag. She usually bikes around the neighborhood or has people drive her. I didn't even know she had her license.

She's wearing a pretty purple dress with a flared skirt and has a bit of a bustier at the front. It's both adorable and devastatingly sexy. Fits right within her brand. Her brown tresses tumble over her shoulders and there is a bow fixed at the back of her head. "It's just Anaheim, Daddy."

Kent lingers on the front porch. "And it's just my car…" he says with a sigh.

"I can take the beamer –"

Kent grins. "I'm just kidding. You're the precious cargo. I don't give a damn about the car."

I smile to myself. I know that feeling. All the stupid things I used to care about, the status symbols like clothes and cars and property, didn't matter anymore once Jessica was born. The second she had a blowout right on a Balmain T-shirt, all of that went right out the window.

Amy bounds back up to her father and kisses his cheek. "I'll be fine, Dad."

I swoon. She's such a sweetheart. I can't help but wish she was rushing to give me a kiss goodbye too. Just a tiny one on the cheek would be enough to make my heart sing for her.

I watch as they say their goodbyes and Kent retreats into the house.

Amy, alone, goes to the Jaguar.

This is the first time I've seen her in the flesh since we kissed. Am I really going to waste the opportunity and let her get away?

I don't have much time to weigh the pros and the cons.

Just have to act. "Morning, Amy!" I call out, rounding the Hummer.

Amy freezes beside the car and looks over at me. Her previously jolly expression falls.

Shit.

"Good morning, Hunter," she replies very formally in an attempt to put me at a distance, but dammit, everything she does is adorable.

Amy reaches for the doorhandle and I panic. I'm not ready to let her go that easily. "Anaheim, huh?"

She freezes and eyes me. "Were you listening to our conversation?"

Dammit, Hunter. I usually can manage a level of smoothness with women. I mean, after all, I do utilize the modern equivalent of a little black book, keeping a few girls on rotation. With Amy, though, all of that is out the window. She makes me nervous. I haven't felt nervous since...well, not since my ex-wife. "Not listening, not at all, just – just couldn't help but overhear," I say adamantly.

She twists her lips to the side. *Likely story.*

"S-so, what are you doing all the way down there?"

Amy sighs as if speaking to me is draining her energy. "I've got a book signing down there."

"Ah, well, that's a perfect place. Maybe someone from Disney will stumble upon you and want to buy up the rights to a Petunia Playpark," I ramble nervously.

To my surprise and delight, Amy smiles. It's subtle, but it's there. "Maybe someday. But today I'm just reading at a local bookstore. Small potatoes."

"Petunia is not small potatoes," I say. If only I could make her truly understand the level of Jessica's obsession. Or mine at this point. She's a genius in my eyes.

Amy becomes suddenly aware she has deigned to smile

at me and presses her lips into a firm line. "Anyway, I should really be going. Traffic and everyth—"

She's cut off when Jessica proudly clomps out the door in her teeny hiking boots and cries out, "Is everything ready for our mission today?"

I smack the hood of the car. "Just warming her up, Captain."

Jessica surveys the landscape hawkishly and then drops the act to skip over to the car.

"Well, you look like a true explorer, Jessica!"

Like a scared deer, Jessica's eyes grow wide and she hurriedly finds a place beside me, wrapping her arms around my leg. You'd think she had never seen Amy in her life or spent hours in the world of Petunia that Amy created.

"What do you say, Jess?"

"Thank you," Jessica squeaks.

I half-laugh. "You know, even explorers can be a little introverted."

"So can grown-ups," Amy says, eyes on Jessica, smiling. "I'm the same way."

Jessica smiles and bashfully turns her face into my leg.

"Okay, let's get this explorer buckled in, huh?" I say, lifting her off the ground and popping her inside the back-seat of the car.

Just as I reach in to help her get buckled, I hear the Jaguar start. *Damn, I wasn't ready.* "Just a sec, Jess," I say before quickly striding over the property line to the Solace driveway. I bend down and wave through the tinted front window. A brief moment passes. Amy can pretend she didn't see me if she wants to.

I start to lift my fist to knock when the window rolls down just a crack. "Do you need something?" Amy asks. I can just see her eyes peeking over the glass.

"Um, yes, sorry, don't mean to hold you up any, I just —" I'd tell myself to get to the point but I don't even know the point. The only thing I'm trying to do is get her to stay a little bit longer. Act like she doesn't hate me. "Would you send along my thanks to Gillian for recommending this camp to us? It's been really great for Jess. She just loves it."

The tension in the corners of her eyes drops, but before I can read her expression any further, she turns her face forward. "Will do."

The window rolls up and the Jaguar clicks into gear, reversing out of the driveway right in front of me.

I watch the entire time as Amy backs out into the road and then speeds down the street until she's just a speck of memory.

Dammit...I really fucked this up.

"Daddy! I'm going to be late for my mission!" Jessica crows.

I jump to attention. My daughter needs me. "So sorry, Captain! On my way!"

Jessica is my first priority. I'll put my feelings in a box and leave them until later. That's my job.

However, that doesn't mean that Amy doesn't crowd my thoughts the entire drive to Jessica's camp nor my day at the office later. In fact, by the end of the day, I'm convinced most of my thoughts have been about Amy Solace.

9

———

AMY

THERE IS NO WEIRDER FEELING THAN BEING HORNY IN my childhood bedroom. It's been a rare occasion ever since puberty.

But ever since Hunter...well, it's constant. I try to push it away, but it won't go.

Resistance is futile.

I've been woken up by a throbbing feeling in my groin on multiple occasions. Now is one of those moments. I don't even know what time it is, but it's still dark out.

And I'm wide awake, blood rushing through me, practically pumping to the beat of his name.

Hunter Ricks, Hunter Ricks, Hunter Ricks.

I haven't changed the decorations much over the years, not since I was sixteen and did a whole overhaul of the Hello Kitty theme I had been committed to as a child. Now, it's all light blue and frilly. Not really the room of a girl in her mid-twenties.

Living at home definitely doesn't help in the intimacy department. The few dating relationships I have had were short-lived and never really manifested in anything more than kissing, groping, maybe humping.

And never here. God, that would feel like a desecration of my childhood room. Not to mention if my father was in the house.

I've never felt these feelings so intensely, though. And I hate myself for them.

I stormed out of Hunter's yard, determined to never waste another moment thinking about him and his stupid pretty face and bulging biceps again.

But in the two weeks since our kiss...kiss*es*...he's all I've thought about.

My body won't let me think about anything else.

Tonight, I smash my eyelids together, determined to just fall back asleep. At least if he appears to me in a dream, it's sort of out of my control. Conjuring images of him to touch myself feels like breaking my determination to push Hunter Ricks far from my mind.

However, images of him are practically tattooed on the back of my eyelids.

I'm totally screwed, aren't I?

I remember his moonlit face, his little smile through his beard, the way his hair hung over his shoulders.

And then...oh god...I can't help but remember how he looked with a towel wrapped around his waist when I barged into his kitchen. I had to turn around so I didn't stare directly at his pelvis. Otherwise, I might have started wishing his towel might fall off.

I don't understand how I can crave sex if I've never had it. But *boy,* do I.

Maybe just once. Indulge myself just once, let the image of Hunter run wild in my brain. Then I can put it to bed. Because I know it will never, ever happen. I won't let it happen. I will never be his second choice.

Sure, he may have been willing to tell his little plaything to leave when I was already there. But then he would have expected a favor for a favor. And while my body was revved up like a race car, I don't know if I would have been ready to give it to him then.

Focus, Amy. He's not here. Don't let his choices ruin your fantasy.

Okay. Fantasy. I can work with fantasy. I'm a writer, aren't I?

Of children's books, dummy.

Sometimes I wonder if I'm a little stunted in my brain. I'm the youngest child, I live at home, I write kids' books, sleep in my childhood bedroom. Maybe I need to grow up.

Jordan would say I'm being mean to myself.

I'm inclined to agree, most of the time.

But then I remember I'm a virgin. And while I don't judge other people for not having sex, I certainly judge myself. Just look at two of my sisters who got pregnant out of wedlock, assumedly because they felt so passionately about having sex with someone that it *had* to happen.

That terrifies me to my core.

Amy. Fantasy time.

Right, right. Nearly let my anxiety be the thing keeping me awake instead of the horniness.

Hunter in a towel. Focus on that.

His pecs glistening from his shower. Dark hair damp over his shoulders. The smell of coffee permeating the room.

I was in my bikini...wonder what he thought of that in the moment.

I hope he liked it.

In my imagination, I am a vixen. I'm not afraid. And so I imagine myself walking toward him instead of squealing away in fear.

My center throbs, calling for my fingers.

"Fine..." I mutter to myself and shove my fingers into my pajama shorts.

Oh, fuck. I'm wet.

Really wet.

We haven't even done anything in my imagination and I'm already a mess.

I imagine Hunter taking me by the hips and pressing me up against the counter, towering over me. His thumbs playing with the elastic of my swim bottoms.

"What are you doing here? Looking like *that*," he growls.

Not sure how I would take to domineering and intimidation in real life, but in a fantasy, god, is it stirring.

I tilt my head back. "What would you like me here for?"

"Is that even a question?"

Hunter seems like he takes control easily, so it comes easily in my fantasy that he'd lift me up onto the counter, ramming his lips into mine and eagerly ripping my bikini bottoms off.

My clit throbs. I let my thumb skim it, my body convulsing at the sensitivity. "Oh, fuck."

Hunter's lips trail down from my mouth to my jaw to my neck. There, he lingers, nipping at the skin hard enough to leave a mark. Luckily, in my imagination, I don't have to worry about explaining that to my dad afterwards.

Stop thinking about your dad, Amy!

Back to Hunter. Hunter's lips tracing my clavicle, moving down to the mount of my breast, slipping his tongue beneath the cup, lapping at the nipple.

My hand between my legs becomes his in my imagination.

"Wet for me, Amy."

God, the way I want him to whisper my name in my ear.

"Want to be inside you..."

And the way I want him to let me know how much he wants *me*. Beg to be inside me.

In my fantasy, it won't hurt. I've heard the first time hurts; some people say it's horrible while others say it's not so bad. With the right person, it wouldn't be so bad. Maybe it would even be pleasurable.

However, as I touch myself to this fantasy, it doesn't hurt at all. Hunter slips inside me as if he was made for me and starts to pulse his hips into me. I wrap myself around him, my ass bouncing across the counter over and over as he pulls our hips flush together and then apart.

My fingers speed up against my clitoris. I point my toes, lock out my knees. I'm close.

"Fuck," he grunts in my ear. "So tight."

He's strong and powerful as he fucks me. I'm not worried about anyone hearing or seeing us; it's a fantasy after all. All I care about is how good it feels to have Hunter fuck me.

"Look at me."

I'm getting so close my clitoris keeps screaming, "Just one more."

I've only ever made myself come and I know how easy that can be when the circumstances are right. My sisters have complained in the past about their conquests, not caring what they were feeling or thinking they had to do the bare minimum to pleasure them.

But Hunter...I can't imagine he would be anything short

of perfect. Girls wouldn't keep coming back to him if he was a lousy lover.

Amy! Don't bring them into it!

Right, right – *Hunter*. Just Hunter.

I bet Hunter Ricks would make me come.

"Look at me when you come."

In my "imagined and will definitely never happen" scenario, he definitely does.

Fantasy and reality collide as my eyes shoot open. Though the reality is I'm lying in my childhood bedroom, unable to fall asleep, the image emblazoned on the insides of my eyelids remains. It's like a hallucination, Hunter's eyes lighting up in front of me.

And the intensity is too much to bear for my sensitive bud.

An orgasm ricochets through my body. So powerful and good that I gasp; I bury my head in the pillow in order to let out a tremendous moan. My forearm burns from working so hard and my whole body shakes for a brief moment before collapsing back into the sheets with exhaustion.

I try to reconjure the fantasy in my brain, but it's too far gone at this point.

The reality is, I'm laying alone in my childhood bedroom and there's no Hunter in sight. He is not the man of my dreams. He is my next door neighbor who is so horny he needs to have girls on tap.

And despite all of that, I can't ignore how not only my body, but my heart, yearn to be his.

"AND...*BOO!*" Stella cries out, popping her face over Tana's baby bouncer.

Tana breaks out into a fit of gurgly laughter, spreading her teeny hands out over her face. It's crazy how big she's gotten in these four months. When Harley told us a week ago she started laughing I could barely believe it.

Now it's music to my ears.

"Aren't you getting tired of that, Stell?" Kira asks. "You want to jump in the pool? Or the swings?" she adds, scanning the unused yard.

Stella ignores Kira, recoiling from Tana's bouncer and then poking her head back in front of the baby. "Boo!"

Again, Tana's melodic, open laugh.

"Guess not," I say softly, just for Kira's ears.

Kira grunts and leans back in her lounge chair. "I want to swim."

"Then you can swim," I reply. "I can look after them. Besides, Stella might follow after you."

Kira checks her smartwatch. "No, it's almost time for dinner. And, if my calculations are correct, Tana is going to start whining for milk soon."

I roll my eyes. Leave it to Kira to "calculate" the needs of a baby as if it's somehow a science. In some ways it is, but nothing can account for temperament and just the general randomness of life. Still, though, I like her spirit to make anything some sort of scientific project. It's just how I see everything as a potential story.

Kira and I have been tasked with babysitting our nieces while Harley and Grant go on a double date with Gillian and Axel. We told them not to worry about coming home at a certain time. After all, what is family for but to babysit the little ones when you need some grown-up time? I just hope when my time comes, they'll do the same.

Who am I kidding? *If* my time comes.

"What's going on, K?" I ask.

Kira eyes me. "What do you mean?"

"You're a bit grumpy, aren't you?"

Kira starts to respond, but is interrupted by Stella teasing Tana with another, "Boo!" She grimaces and crosses her arms over her chest. "What makes you think that?"

I laugh. Kira has been the quiet one our whole lives. But since the rest of our sisters moved out, we've become closer than close. I've heard Kira talk more over the past few years than our entire childhood. "I don't know...maybe the crossed arms? The sour face?"

Kira touches her cheek and realizes her lips are down-turned. "Oh..."

"So. Now that you can't hide from me..."

"Amy, it's fine. Really."

"Please! You're hanging out with the three coolest people you know and you look like you're at a funeral."

Kira smirks. "Coolest isn't the word I'd use."

"Boo!" Stella shouts. Tana laughs.

I smile at the scene. Coolest might not be the word Kira would use, but it's the one I would use. Watching my sisters become mothers has been one of the most rewarding things to watch. Not to mention watching my nieces grow up from day one up to now. What could be cooler than growing? Changing? For the better, of course.

"Work stuff," Kira finally says. "Boring."

"Just because I don't understand what you do doesn't mean I find it boring." Admittedly, there have been times I've accidentally tuned her out while she rants and raves about whatever she does at her engineering job. Forgive me that I don't understand a good chunk of the words she throws around. The curse of being the smartest person I know, I guess. "Besides, you're not usually so...sullen about work things."

"Sullen...that's why you're the writer."

I snort. "Sullen isn't that special of a word."

"I wouldn't ever use the word sullen to describe anything. *Writer*," she repeats adamantly.

I resist qualifying that with, "Of kids' books." It's valid. How do people learn to read without children's books? At least this is what Jordan would say to me.

"I have a new boss," Kira says.

Oof. Kira hates change already. That's why she's the very logical, left-brained one. She likes that facts, figures, and physics don't change just because we feel like it. "Okay..."

"And he's...I don't like him."

"What'd he do?"

Kira's lips twist to the side. "Nothing."

I resist laughing.

"Nothing yet. But I just know...I just know he's going to do something that's going to piss me off."

"Okay, are you a psychic, or –"

"He's Trevor's son."

I know Trevor. Trevor is the CEO of Wynters Corp. Or should I say former CEO since now his son has taken over, apparently. Kira has always sung his praises. He was the one to take a chance on her and pull her into a male dominated company, allowed her to take the reins on projects and always backed her up when her male coworkers trounced her work. "Look, nepotism –"

"It's not the nepotism that bothers me. Well, maybe a little. I mean, Orlie's worked at the company for years, so –"

"*Orlie?!!*"

Kira chuckles. "Yeah. Short for Orlando."

"I'm sorry, Orlie is a stupid name," I reply.

"You always know how to make me feel better," she says.

"Okay, sorry, just – Orlie, wow. I..." I sigh. Rich people and their crazy names. It's not like we don't come from money ourselves, but at least none of us are named Orlie. "Anyway, what's your problem with...Orlie."

Kira shrugs. "I've just got a bad feeling about him. I don't think he really knows what he's doing."

"You said he works at the company, so –"

"Yeah, but it's different. He's just younger, and I just don't think he has the drive or focus that Trevor has ever had."

I smile sympathetically. "Maybe you can give him a month or so to prove you wrong?"

"No," Kira replies curtly.

My eyebrows jump. "Okay...."

"I mean...sorry, I just –" She shifts in her seat. "I have a bad feeling about it. That's all. And I can't shake it."

With Kira, it's important to wait for her to ask for advice before you give it to her. That was my mistake. I'll lay off and let her come to me with her problems as they arise. For now, though, she just needs a sister to hear her thoughts and say, "That sucks." So, that's what I say. "That sucks."

Kira nods. "Yeah. It does."

While the world is still alight with California twilight, the mood between us is rather dull now.

"I know what will fix this. Pizza. I'm going to order the pizza," Kira says, clapping her hands on her thighs and getting to her feet. "What do you want, Ames?"

"Mushroom, pepperoni, and olive."

Kira pulls a face. "Okay, one disgusting pizza for you and, Stella –'"

"Just cheese!" Stella chirps. Tana giggles again and

Stella digs her fingers against Tana's cheeks, repeating, "Cheese, cheese, cheese!"

"Great, so three pizzas to satiate our eclectic taste," Kira says.

"Satiate *and* eclectic? Are you sure you aren't the writer in this family?"

Kira laughs, readjusting her glasses as she heads back inside.

I sit for a bit and watch Stella and Tana. I could get lost in it for hours. Kids...they're just so special. I wonder to myself if I'll ever have my own little one to complement this picture. Hard to imagine, given my lack of experience in the bedroom, that I'll ever get to that point. But my body wants that. So bad.

My reverie is broken by the sound of the doorbell. I look over my shoulder through the screen door. Kira bolts off in the direction of the front door. "I'll get it."

Who could be coming by so late? Did Dad forget his key? Is the double date over already due to some unforeseen error? Neither of those make a good deal of sense.

I stand up from my chair and go to the door, looking over at Stella and Tana from time to time to make sure they're alright. I watch as Kira clasps her hand on the doorknob and throws the door open.

My stomach drops when I see the man towering over her.

What the hell is Hunter Ricks doing here?

10

HUNTER

When Kira answers the door, I can't help but be the tiniest bit disappointed.

Jessica heard Stella's voice and the tiny giggling of Harley's baby before I did. And when I peered out an upstairs window, I watched the scene for a little too long to not be considered creepy. Kira and Amy sitting beside the pool, little Tana in her baby bouncer and Stella making crazy faces to get her to laugh.

I've thought about Amy every day, all day since we kissed. It's gotten to the point where I know I *have* to do something about it. I just don't know how to get her alone. How to tell her. Especially when she's avoiding me. I never see her out drawing in the yard anymore and, if she leaves through the front door, she scurries, clearly not wanting to be bothered.

I don't want to make her uncomfortable. But I can't stand living with the feeling in the pit of my stomach that if I don't shoot my shot, I'll die regretting it.

Of course, when Jessica asked if we could go over and

ask to play, I wasn't going to refuse. It's like the girl can read my mind.

No hesitation. Didn't even bat an eye. Just grabbed my daughter's hand and marched right over to the front door of the Solace house. I didn't bother to pay attention to my pounding heart or all the second thoughts I was having.

Is this creepy? Should I stop?

Nope. Didn't let those questions run my mind for even a second.

Until right now when I'm face to face with Kira and I realize that this interest in Amy is turning into an obsession. I'm going to be the creepy next door neighbor in no time flat if I keep this up.

Lucky for us, Kira's surprise is overshadowed by her smile, apples of her cheeks tightening. "Hi guys! What's up?"

My mouth is dry. I can't seem to form words. And Jessica isn't one of those precocious kids, like Stella Solace. She isn't going to speak for me. "I – I'm –" *You're over forty years old, dude. Get it together.* "We heard you all in the backyard and –"

"Oh, I'm sorry, are we being too loud?" Kira says, wincing.

"No, Jessica just wanted to know if there was room for one more to…" I trail off; over Kira's shoulder, I can see straight through the Solace house, through the kitchen to the screen door that leads out onto their patio. And there in the door is Amy, staring back at me, her eyebrows folded in confusion. I suddenly feel very stupid for this whole thing.

"Of course!" Kira answers without me having to finish my sentence. *Thank god.* "I'm just about to order dinner. You could join us out in the backyard for a bit and then, if you like, stay for pizza too."

I feel Jessica tug on my hand. I look down at her, find her hazel eyes and hopeful smile. "Only if we're not imposing," I reply to Kira.

"Not at all! What are neighbors for?"

Well, it's clear Amy hasn't said anything to Kira. Or if she has, Kira thinks Amy's opinion is wrong and now she's encouraging us to be closer. I can't imagine that's the case. What kind of sister would she be if she wasn't on Amy's side? I don't have siblings, so I have no idea what that feels like, but I'd have to imagine there is some sort of solidarity involved.

"Come on, Jessica. Stella will be so excited to see you. She'll teach you how to make Tana laugh," Kira says, giving Jessica a "come on" gesture and starting off through the house.

Jessica starts to follow, still holding tight to my hand. We follow Kira through the Solace house to the screen door; Amy has disappeared from the doorway and is now sitting back in a lounge, acting nonplussed.

"We've got a visitor!" Kira announces.

Stella looks up and grins. "Hi Jess!"

Jessica finally lets go of my hand and hurries over to Stella. I'm grateful that, despite the age difference, Stella and Jessica manage to get on just great. Stella's a good kid, always making sure Jessica is keeping up. I hope they're friends for a long time.

"Well, two visitors," Kira corrects herself. "Amy, say hi."

Amy looks over at me through big black sunglasses. "Oh, hi Hunter."

Oh, hi Hunter?! As if she didn't just see me through the door? "Amy. Good to see you."

She hesitates for half a second. No one else would notice it. But I'm hyper aware of literally everything Amy does, so of course I notice the chasm of her silence and fall so deep into it I'm afraid I'll never come up for air. "You too," she replies and then looks in the direction of the girls who are now both seated on their bottom in front of Tana, tickling her feet.

Out of the corner of my eye, Kira starts to move back toward the door to go inside. And I can't let that happen. Because I need to talk to Amy alone. Not alone in front of the children. *Alone* alone. I've been thinking about her too much to let things go on like this any longer. "Amy! Would it be alright if I talked to you for a moment?"

The world seems to stop for a second as she turns to look at me.

"Privately?" I add, sending a nervous look over to Kira.

Kira stops on her trajectory toward the door and glances at Amy.

"Um. Sure." She gets up off the lounge, her long summer dress sliding down her legs like water. I swallow, thinking about my own hands trailing up her tanned calves and thighs. "Inside?"

Amy starts to go before I can answer. I tuck my hands into my pockets and say, to no one in particular, "Sounds good."

I follow Amy into the house, shuffling past Kira who is eyeing me with curiosity. I smile awkwardly. My heart throbs in my chest, beating with every step like a drum, drowning out every other sound.

My eyes are trained on Amy as we walk further into the house, through the kitchen and into the front room, the kind no one ever uses except for when they have company they aren't sure what to do with. Is that what I am to her? Just someone she needs to entertain for a moment?

If that's how she feels now, I'm determined to change her mind in the next few minutes.

Amy, however, doesn't sit on one of the white settees. She simply crosses her arms and turns to me. She looks smaller than small, the way she's caving in on herself. "What do you want, Hunter?"

I lick my lower lip and consider her expression. Eyes stuck on the floor between us. Pretty pink lips downturned. My eyes fall slightly lower and I see her nipples poking out through the fabric of her dress. *Fuck, that's so...* I have to snap out of it. This isn't about *sex*. Well, it's not *not* about sex. But it's not about that exclusively.

My feelings are so much more. My heart feels connected to her.

I need to tell her.

"I owe you an apology for..." I begin but fail to find the right words to encapsulate what exactly I'm apologizing for.

Amy lifts her head and smiles sadly, "It's fine, Hunter. Seriously. It was a mistake. I'm over it."

I blink. "It wasn't a mistake," I say, though my voice tremors.

Amy stares back at me. "What?"

"It wasn't –" I clear my throat. "It wasn't a mistake. At least to me."

Amy shakes her head, soft brown curls swaying. "Hunter –"

"It wasn't a mistake to me because I've never felt like this before."

She takes a small step back from me, frowning. "Hunter, are you feeling alright?"

"No, I'm not, but it's not because I'm not in my right mind or, or –" *Fuck, why isn't this coming out right.* "I can't stop thinking about you, Amy."

Amy's brown eyes widen. "Um…"

"Just hear me out. Five minutes. Please."

She doesn't speak. Doesn't react. Just waits.

Okay. This is it, Hunter. This is all you get. Make it count. "That kiss…my intention wasn't to rope you into some one-night stand with me. Or use you. Nothing like that. It was – it was impulsive."

She frowns.

"But that doesn't mean it was thoughtless!" I add quickly and then realize my voice is growing too loud. *Deep breath. Stay calm.* "It was…I was expressing exactly what I felt for you in that moment. What I *feel* for you." A wave of emotion runs through me, so intense I can almost feel my body undulate with it. "I couldn't have planned for it to happen that way. And I understand how awful it must have felt to know that another woman showed up just moments after."

Amy winces.

"I didn't mean to betray you. I didn't. But I know I did, and for that, I'm sorry."

"I don't want to talk about this, Hunter."

A knife to the heart. But it doesn't kill me. "I don't mean to make it worse, but –"

"You *are* making it worse!" she murmurs, words tight between her lips. "I don't want to be reminded of all the women you could have with the snap of your fingers. I'm not one of them."

"You're not!" I agree. "That's just it! You're not that at all."

Amy scoffs. "Wow, thanks."

"No, that's not –" Fuck, we're misunderstanding each other. This is going terribly. "I'd never expect that of you. Because you're not one of them, you're – you're –" All of the women I have had relationships with are worthy of love and attention from a man that isn't me. They know that. That's always been clear. We do our thing, we have our fun, and then we go about our lives.

"What am I, Hunter? Easy? Right next door? Someone to have fun with whose Uber you don't have to pay for? What am I?"

"Oh my god, Amy, you're driving me fucking insane," I reply. It's twofold. She's been driving me crazy for weeks now. And right now, she's driving me nuts because she won't let me say what I need to say. Although I can't seem to even *say* what I need to say.

I have to act. I have to show her.

Before Amy can make another retort, I grab her by the back of the head and kiss her hard, as deep as I can without delving my tongue into her mouth and letting her know exactly how deep I want to be inside her.

She lets out an exclamation of surprise against my mouth but doesn't pull away. One of her hands rests against my chest and I feel her pelvis move toward mine.

Don't get hard, Hunter. This is not the time.

My hand loops through the soft waves of her hair. I can't resist touching her soft cheek. I knew I wanted this badly, but having this need met is even better than I could have possibly imagined.

Amy's lips roll against mine. Her fingers curl into my T-shirt.

She needs me too. I can feel it.

Her lips fall away from mine, but she does not pull away. I could easily close the few inches between us again, however, that would mean I couldn't look into her beautiful brown eyes that make my heart sing. "Hunter –"

"I *feel* something for you, Amy. Bigger than just a kiss.

Bigger than anything like that," I say. Finally, I get out of my own way and say what I actually mean.

Amy's lips curl upward, but she shakes her head. "I'm not going to be one of your girls, Hunter."

"You wouldn't be," I say, sliding my hands down the sides of her head, tucking pieces of hair out of her face. "You would be the only one, Amy. *The only one.*"

Her jaw falls. There. I got through to her.

Now I just need to wait for her answer.

"H-how can I be sure?" she asks.

I understand her apprehension. I haven't shown her the type of man I am. Have wanted to be but have been stopped from becoming. "I can only prove it to you with my actions. If you'll let me. I'd like to...I'd like to try for something more."

"Why me? What makes me any different than –"

"Everything," I answer without thinking. "That lifestyle worked for me with those women. But I'm tired of it. I want more. With you."

Amy is silent, eyes wide, trapped in mine.

She isn't convinced. That's okay, though. I only need the chance to try. "You don't have to trust me all at once, but...but would you let me try?" I ask, tucking my hand against her chin. "Let me take you out. And show you what kind of man I am."

To my delight, Amy smiles again, raises herself up on her tiptoes, kisses my cheek, lips brushing through my beard. "Alright," she whispers before she retreats. "I'll let you try."

I feel faint.

Before I can pull her back into me for kiss after kiss after *kiss*, Amy breaks away from me. "We should get back to them before they start to worry or...or wonder."

I am frozen in place, watching her go, not really believing what has just happened.

"Hunter, are you coming?" Amy asks with a smile thrown toward me over her shoulder.

Now that I've let all my thoughts go, I don't seem to be able to stop them. "I'm just enjoying watching you walk away."

Her smile turns into a grin. "Well, enjoy, then." She leaves, hips swaying gently, curls bouncing.

I tighten my fist in the air. I've done it. I've gotten my chance.

And I'm going to hold on as tight as I can.

Hope you're having a good day. I'm
thinking about you.

I HAVE REREAD THE TEXT THIS ENTIRE CAR RIDE. IN
fact, every text or email he's sent me I've read over and over
again, trying to pick them apart, find reasons why I
shouldn't let myself fall deeper into Hunter Ricks.

I haven't found a reason to pull away yet.

Except for one simple fact.

We've been at this texting game for a week straight and
there's been no talk of an actual date. None. And I'm not
going to be the one to suggest it. *He's* the one who has to
prove himself, not me.

Plus...I'm not sure how I would even go about asking or
planning such a thing. I'm shy, remember?

"Who is he?"

I lift my head and look at Fiona in the driver's seat.
"Huh?"

Fiona smiles glancing at me from the driver's seat as we
speed down Ventura Boulevard. "You're staring at your

phone like you could kiss it and have a big stupid smile on your face. Who is he?"

I turn off the screen on my phone and tuck it between my thighs. "No one."

"Uh-huh. Likely story."

"Fiona…"

"Come on! It's not often I get to probe you about your love life."

I give her a side eye. "Why? Because it's non-existent?"

Fiona hesitates. "You said it, not me."

I laugh. For once, it's not. For once, it's very real. Well, almost. "We're just talking right now."

"How'd you meet him?"

I bite the inside of my cheek. "Um. Mutual friend."

"Sounds suspicious."

"Listen –"

"Kidding, kidding." Fiona is quiet for a moment. "You only have to tell me what you want to. I'm not going to pry."

Fiona is a friend and she's also a bit like a surrogate mom on occasions. Like a cool mom who would let you drink in her basement when you're underage. "There's not a lot to tell." *Liar.* "We just have been talking a little bit. Nothing is happening."

"You haven't gone on a date?"

I sigh. "He hasn't even asked me out."

"Oh, honey. How old is he?"

"Um…older than me."

Fiona raises an eyebrow. "How much older than you?"

"Let's just say older than me."

She nods as if she understands completely, which, given Fiona's world-weariness, I wouldn't be surprised if she does. "Well, if you're going to date an older man, he's at least gotta be mature."

"True."

"What's the point otherwise? You shouldn't be trapped in the talking phase with someone older than you. That's a red flag."

I gulp. "Red flag?"

"Yeah. Like he's just trying to pass the time."

I've tried to hold tight to Hunter's words and actions from the last time I saw him. He seemed to be adamant. Felt so adamant in the way he kissed me. I've justified his lack of planning as the downside of dating (seeing? Talking with?) a very busy man. I can't rush him. He's older. Way more established. Maybe he's trying to figure out how to fit me in his schedule.

"It might be sweet, Amy, but words won't keep you warm at night," Fiona says pointedly.

"I know, I know..." I grumble and lean on the door to watch the city pass by.

Fiona sighs. "Sorry, I don't mean to be a downer. As long as you're having fun, that's all that matters."

I don't know if I'm having fun. I know if Hunter stopped sending me sweet messages it would break my heart. But how long can I live on sweet messages and well wishes? None of that is real or tangible. How many more women does he send these to?

You have to trust, Amy. You have to trust or else you'll ruin it for yourself.

It's not like I've been blessed in the *trusting* department. After all, my mother left our family not once but twice. The only people I've ever trusted are my sisters. And my dad. But after Mom left, even that was in question. What if he left too? I thought my parents couldn't leave and then one of them did. What would stop Dad?

I've worked through that in therapy. Dad is Dad. He'd never do that. And he didn't. *Doesn't.*

Can I afford to trust another man?

Maybe.

"Here we are..." Fiona says in my silence.

The bookstore appears on the right, Gregor's Worldly Words in Sherman Oaks. It's just the usual. A reading and then a signing for local parents and kids. I'm starting to get tired of toting this volume of Petunia around. Reading it used to be cathartic. Now it's just a reminder of my tragic backstory. And then I remember the next Petunia I haven't even started writing because I can't seem to nail down an idea for it.

"Now to find parking..." Fiona drawls.

That's why, in LA, you arrive a half hour before you have to be anywhere. Of course, that is if you care about being on time.

THE READING GOES GREAT. I don't get any weird looks from parents this time which is a first. In fact, I think word has gotten round about what this book is really about and it seems that the communities that need it are showing up in droves. I see a lot of single parents here with their kids, smiling to themselves.

That's a nice feeling. As much as this book is for kids, it's for parents too. Of course, not my mom. My mom didn't leave only to stick around. But if I can aid in parents being able to explain their big life changes to their children, then I've done a good job.

The signing is a record breaker, at least for me. I think

every person who came for the reading stays to get a copy. By the last ten people, my hand is aching.

"Just a couple more, Ames," Fiona says, patting my back.

I toss my hair out of my eyes and take a deep breath as I reach for another book. I open it up to the inside cover. "Who can I make this out to?" I ask without looking.

"Um…" a man's deep voice replies.

I look up and am stunned to see Hunter standing in front of the signing table. He's not in his usual T-shirt and jeans, but in a nice linen suit, his long hair tied back in a serious looking bun. "What are you doing here?"

Hunter chuckles nervously. "You seem upset I'm here."

"I'm – no, I'm not –" I stop short when I see the bustling bouquet of white chrysanthemums and yellow snapdragons.

"Holy shit," I hear Fiona mutter.

She's going to have a lot of questions later, that's for sure.

"Hi!" I finally say and get to my feet.

Hunter beams.

I round the table and go to him, unsure of whether to hug him or…

Luckily, he takes the reins and kisses my cheek in a friendly, yet lingering way. "That was great," he says.

"You were here? During the reading?" I ask in shock. He's a hard guy to miss. Surely, I would have seen him amidst the crowd of tiny humans.

"I was, although I was kind of hiding in the stacks," he says shyly, nodding toward some of the shelves of books. "I didn't want to throw you off your game."

"Shouldn't you be at work?" I continue my line of questioning. I'm trying not to let myself become totally ensconced with wonder, but I can't help it. This is one of the sweetest things imaginable.

He shrugs. "It's my company."

"Of course," I giggle.

We both fall quiet for a moment. Thank god he was at the end of the line, so we don't have anyone left to care about. Because I am *truly* getting lost in his burning brown eyes. How can a man be so darling and so sexy at once?

"Oh – uh – these are for you," Hunter says, pushing the bouquet toward me. "Obviously."

I take it tenderly. "Not so obvious..." I say with a sneaking smile.

Hunter blushes underneath his beard. "Well, it should be obvious."

I'm not ready to stop giving him shit for his antics. Until I know for sure I'm his one and only, I will hold his feet to the fire. Still though. Flowers...that's a nice touch. "They're beautiful." I inhale deeply. "Mm. Thank you."

"You're welcome. You deserve many more flowers than that for your performance but –"

I laugh. "It's not a performance, it's just a reading."

Hunter stops and smiles. "Well, it was amazing."

His voice is so earnest I'm having a hard time *not* believing him.

"Listen, I hate to run –"

And there goes the air out of my balloon.

"But I've got a meeting in a half hour and have to make it back to the office and, well, anyway –"

I touch one of the flowers, feeling the velvety petals between my fingers, hoping it will calm me. "Yeah, I get it."

"I want to take you out this weekend."

Well, that was unexpected. I swear I hear Fiona squeal over my shoulder. "This weekend?"

"With Jess, if that's alright. I know that leaves some romance to be desired, but –"

My heart swells. He wouldn't invite me on a date with Jessica if he didn't trust me around her. That's more of a compliment than he even knows. "No, that's perfect."

He smiles. "Okay. The beach."

"Love the beach."

"Picnic."

"*Love* a picnic."

Hunter's smile grows with each moment. "Sunday. Afternoon?"

"Love Sunday afternoon," I say and am surprised when Hunter says it in unison with me. I flush. "Am I that predictable?"

"No, not at all," he replies and then leans into my ear. "But you are adorable."

I could die happy right now, but then I'd miss our date. Gotta hold on to life support a few days more.

Hunter touches my shoulder gingerly, another kiss to the side of my head. "Alright, I've got to be going."

"I'm Fiona, *by the way*," Fiona interjects, holding her hand out to Hunter.

He shakes it, a sheepish look on his face. "Forgive me, Fiona, I was d-distracted."

"I can't blame you. She's a catch. A real catch, and if you do anything to –"

"*Fiona*," I admonish.

Hunter holds up his hands in surrender. "Don't worry. I know I'll have you and all the Solace sisters to contend with." Then, his warm brown eyes meet mine, crow's feet deep in a smile. "I'll take good care of her."

What the hell, man? Do you want me to rip all my clothes off right this second? We're in public!

"Hm. Good," Fiona sniffs.

I want to slug her in the arm.

"Nice to meet you, Fiona. And...have a good rest of your day," Hunter says as he backs away.

"You too. Have a good meeting and, you know, day. Have a good day," I call after him.

"Sunday," he says as confirmation.

I nod. "Sunday."

"Good." With that, he gives me one last smile, and then hurries out of the shop. I watch him all the way to the door, the bell tolling on his way out as a warning that I have well and truly lost it.

Fiona touches my shoulder as I zone out. "Okay, looks like you got a date. I give you permission to well and truly lose your shit over this man."

My heart flutters. I clutch the bouquet to my chest as tight as I can without crushing the flowers. What Fiona doesn't know is I've already lost my shit over Hunter Ricks. I lost it long ago, before it was even reasonable.

Now, I've lost my whole self in him too.

Sunday cannot come fast enough.

12

HUNTER

"I think I'm having a panic attack."

"You are *not* having a panic attack," Axel replies over the phone.

"I said *'think'*, didn't I?" I hiss, pacing back and forth in my kitchen. I eye the picnic basket on the counter. "God, what if she doesn't like my cooking?"

Axel chuckles. "Then you go to Malibu Farms."

"You're not helping," I retort.

"I'm sorry! I'm just trying to help you calm down."

I shake my head. "I don't think I'm going to calm down."

"Just think about it being over, then. That's what I always think about when I have big presentations or –"

"Well, I don't want it to be over! It hasn't even fucking started!" I immediately seal my lips together and look over my shoulder to make sure Jessica hasn't snuck into the kitchen while I wasn't looking and didn't overhear me say a naughty word.

I can hear Axel is smiling. "That's a good thing, Hunter. That means you're excited."

I guess that's true. With the women I was seeing before

Amy, I never felt nervous. I didn't feel excited either. I was happy to get some release, but other than that, I was not *feeling* much. Now that I'm getting ready for my first official date with Amy (daughter in tow) I'm going batshit crazy with nerves. That's a good sign, right? Means I care.

"You're going to enjoy it. Amy is a sweet girl. She's not going to make it hard for you."

"It's just...I haven't done this in a long time."

"Sounds like me a couple months ago," Axel mutters.

I stop and look out the kitchen window at the Solace house. I wonder if Amy's as nervous as I am. Rushing around, picking out the right outfit, brushing her beautiful, flowing locks, thinking about me thinking about her. "How did you stop being nervous about it?"

"Didn't. Just *did* it. Gillian made it easy."

"You two also had a history," I grumble. "And have known each other many –"

"Doesn't matter how long you know someone. *Dating* them for the first time still comes with all those pre-date jitters. In fact, it might be worse because you really don't want to fuck it up. Doubly worse for me since I fucked it up the first time."

Okay, Axel has a point. He did leave Gillian high and dry back in the day after their short summer fling and didn't even know Stella was his until just this year. He's making up for a lot. "It's just...I know how to flirt."

"I know you know how to flirt."

"I know how to be charming."

"Hell yeah, you do!" Axel replies. I hear Gillian in the background admonish him for his use of the word 'hell'. "...heck yeah, you do."

I chuckle. A welcomed comedic respite from the terror I'm feeling. "I don't know how to do the rest of it, though."

"Yes, you do. You've done it before."

I wince. "A long time ago."

"Doesn't matter. Don't sell yourself short. You're capable of being more than just a fling to someone, Hunter."

I guess that's what this boils down to. I'm not afraid of making Amy a fling. I'm afraid that's all she'll see me as. She'll get past that first layer and realize all I am is fun. A good time. Not a long time. I know what Amy deserves. And I know that I want Amy. But I'm not sure I deserve her.

"What if this doesn't work?" I ask.

"It might not."

I roll my eyes. "Wow, thanks."

"I'm being real with you. It might not. Doesn't mean you shouldn't try."

I check my watch and realize I'm running out of time. It's almost time to walk up to Amy's front door and get her. Thank god she lives next door. For once it's a blessing, not a curse.

"Besides, you're not without a paddle if Amy's not the one. You can always...go back, you know?"

Gillian snaps at him again. "What? I'm not saying he should, I'm saying if!" Axel replies defensively.

There's a skirmish over the phone and then my ear is greeted with Gillian's voice. "Hunter? It's Gillian."

"Hi, Gillian," I say. Now I'm sweating. Talking with a Solace sister about this is more terrifying than I could have imagined.

"If you like my sister as much as you say you do, you're going to delete all those girls in your phone right now."

I am at a loss for words. The numbers in my phone are like a security blanket. I haven't used them since the night I kissed Amy. And that night was the first time I'd used it since she called me out in her bikini. And even that girl got sent packing. I know I just want Amy, but it is comforting knowing they're there. If I get rid of them, who knows what can happen to me.

"Did you hear me?"

"Y-yes, but –"

"Nope! No buts. If you don't want to be a playboy, you need to act like you're not a playboy," she says firmly.

I've never heard Gillian be so direct with me. Usually, she's tenderly walking me through some parenting advice and patting me on the shoulder. "Okay," I squeak.

"Okay?"

"Y-yes. I'll delete them."

There's another struggle over the phone; Axel is once again the one in my ear. "Yo, don't listen to her, she's a biased party in this."

"It's okay, I think she's..." I take a deep breath. "I think she's right."

Axel doesn't reply.

"If I'm serious about this, then I have to act like it."

"Whatever works for you, man," he replies cautiously. "Just remember, you're great. You're Hunter Ricks. Just be yourself, and if it's meant to be..."

It will be.

I check my watch once again. Gametime. "Hey, thanks a lot, man, but I have to go."

"Of course. Let me know how it goes after."

"Sure. And thank Gillian for me too."

"Don't give her too much credit, it'll go to her head!"

I hear Gillian's laughter through the phone. Fills my chest with warmth to hear the two of them together. Gives me some sort of hope for myself.

We say our goodbyes, and as soon as I hang up, Jessica skips through the kitchen. "It's time, Daddy!"

"Give me just one second, Jess," I say, but she's off like a bullet, out the front door, down the steps, and over to Amy's.

Shit.

I don't have much time. It's now or never.

I pull up my contact list and one by one, work through all the mononym contacts. *Brianna...Caitlyn...Jessenia...Molly...*

Each one I delete. No second thought. All gone.

When I reach the last name, Yasmin, and I press the red-fonted "Delete Contact", I feel lighter than air. I never anticipated that getting rid of these names in my phone would be so freeing. But now, those names, numbers, and faces that were cramming the edges of my brain all disappear. And everything, truly this time, is Amy.

"Daddy! Hurry up! We're ready!"

I look up to see Jessica's head poking through the front door. Slowly, Amy appears over her, hair done in two plaits down her shoulders, face glowing with the kiss of shiny sunscreen. Her lips are curled in a serene smile.

My heart grows at the sight of her. "On my way, girls," I say, swiping the picnic basket off the counter and heading toward the front door.

Let's do this.

"I DIDN'T KNOW you could cook, Hunter," Amy remarks, taking a final bite of a potato salad from her plate.

"Daddy's a *great* cook," Jessica announces.

"It's just potato salad," I say shyly.

Amy shakes her head. "Don't be modest. I can barely boil an egg."

I laugh. "Is that so?"

"Not that I'd want to. Hard boiled eggs make me sick."

"Yeah, me too! Blech!" Jessica announces.

I eye my little girl. It's cute when she's trying to get people to like her. I know for a fact she loves hard boiled eggs. But this whole afternoon, she's been trying to be like Amy. Sitting like her, putting the same things on the plate as her even if she won't eat it all. She even asked Amy to braid her hair the same way. Now the two of them are like darling twins.

If there's one thing I like more than liking Amy myself, it's Jessica liking Amy.

"I want to go swimming," Jessica says, looking out at the wide Malibu beach.

"You need to digest for a bit, Jessie," I say. "Maybe make a sandcastle instead."

Jessica harrumphs. "But I want to go swimming."

"Just half an hour."

"That's so *lonnnng*," Jessica complains.

"Tell you what," Amy says, pulling out her phone. "How about you try and make the biggest sandcastle you can in fifteen minutes?"

Jessica's hazel eyes grow big and she smiles.

"Then after fifteen minutes, we'll come to help you make it even bigger. I'll set a timer on my phone and everything. In no time, we'll get to splash in the water."

I try not to swoon at how easily Amy interacts with Jessica. She makes parenting look so easy and she's not even a parent herself.

"Okay! Don't look, though. I want it to be a surprise," Jessica says and leaps to her feet, running to a patch of sand not too far away. Immediately, she starts digging like a dog looking for a bone.

Amy and I both laugh as sand flies through the air.

We're alone now.

For the first time since the date started, we're alone.

Not completely, of course. Jessica is only ten feet away.

But it's more than before.

"Thank you for inviting me today," Amy says, a lovely lilt to her voice. "It's the perfect day for a beach picnic."

"It is, isn't it?" I say, stretching out my legs and leaning back on my palms. "I know Jessica doesn't make it easy to, um, have a *normal* date, but –"

She grins and shakes her head. "It's perfect. I'm having a great time."

I swallow into a smile. "Good. I'm glad."

Amy eyes my hand and then shifts herself to sit next to me. She leans herself back on her palms, just like me, but one of her fingers grazes mine delicately. My whole body feels like it's been hit with an electric shock. Did she do that on purpose? I'm not sure.

"She's a great kid, Hunter," she says.

Damn, she just knows how to hit all the tender parts of my heart. "You're sweet."

"I mean it. She's just..." Amy trails off and watches Jessica take an armful of wet sand over to her castle. "Darling."

"You should see her when she's hangry."

Amy laughs. "You should see *me* when I'm hangry. Not a pretty sight."

"I'm sure you're pretty no matter what."

She laughs and rolls her eyes. "Flatterer."

I bite my lower lip. *Okay, Hunter. You know how to be charming. Don't rest on your laurels.* I shift my hand closer to hers, a few fingers resting on the back of her hand. "You know, Amy, my life is inherently also Jessica's."

"I know."

"So...we're kind of a package deal."

"Don't worry, I understand."

"What I mean is –" I turn to look at her, losing the compulsion to speak when I see how the sun reflects off the amber flecks in her irises. *You have to say it, Hunter.* "Seeing me is like seeing her too. I'll always do my best to make you feel adored and...and special, of course, but she's –"

"Your world."

Wow, she just took the words out of my mouth.

Amy slips her hand out from under mine and before I can be disappointed, she puts it right back on top, squeezing my entire hand. "I love that about you."

The word love...is scary this early. And while she isn't saying she loves me; she's saying she loves something about me.

That's big. To my heart at least. I haven't heard someone say they love something about me other than my dick in a long time.

"I wouldn't want to be a part of your life if I couldn't also be a part of Jessica's. I want her in my life too, I promise," Amy murmurs.

I watch Jessica for a moment. She's completely engrossed, trying to form towers that keep falling from the dryness of the sand. But she is determined, her tongue sticking out of her mouth as she's deep in thought.

While my daughter is distracted, I lean over toward Amy and plant a kiss on her bare shoulder. Her skin is warm and sun-kissed. Her breath tickles my scalp. "I think you're an amazing woman," I say, raising my head.

"You barely know me," she says with a smirk.

I could kiss Amy for real. She's only an inch away. But I want to leave some anticipation. "I know. I barely know you and I already think you're amazing. I can't imagine how truly wonderful you'll be to me when I get to know all of you."

Her eyes flash with fear, but only for a moment. Amy sits up a little straighter, a smug smile on her lips. "Oh. That's nice."

I chuckle. Amy is shy. Parts of her are locked away. And I'm determined to find them out. On her own time, though. I'd never rush her.

I'll wait for Amy as long as I have to.

So I can get to know every single part of her. From the hollows of her heart to those of her body.

I'm determined to make her mine as much as I'm determined to be hers.

"Can you help?! I'm stuck!" Jessica cries out, waving her hand.

"Guess I was too optimistic with those fifteen minutes, huh?" Amy says and starts to get to her feet. "Shall we?"

I smile. "Definitely."

We spend the rest of the afternoon crafting a sandcastle and splashing in the tide. I try not to stare at Amy's beautiful, bikini-clad body. However, it's her smiles that encapsulate my heart. Yes. Plural. One she keeps for herself, one for Jessica, and one for me.

I need that smile as long as she'll let me have it.

13

___

AMY

It's a perfect August night for a barbecue. The backyard is teeming with people. Old friends and new have come out for my twenty-fifth birthday party. All my sisters, their friends and partners, Dad's friends old and new. Even Victoria Neville, Grant's sister and world famous super-model, has managed to slink in although conspicuousness is not really her strong suit. She's poised under a lacy parasol, big sunglasses over her eyes that make her look like a bug.

Of course, the one person that matters, or should I say the *two*, have yet to make their entrance.

I've been seeing Hunter (and Jessica) for nearly a month now. And somehow, he keeps surprising me in the best ways. Though we are accompanied by Jessica on most of our dates (okay, *all*) I feel closer to him than ever. We have gone to dinner, the movies, walks, mini golf, hikes; the list is endless. Ever since our first beach date, he's made time for me.

And Jessica has been a good buffer. Apart from being such a dear, precious child, she has assured me that Hunter isn't just in this for my body.

He wants more.

And, almost perversely, that's made me want more from him.

From the longing gazes over bonfires in his backyard while we make s'mores with Jess (while my family was out, of course) to the subtle brush of his hand or stolen kisses while Jessica isn't looking, my body has sunk further and further into desperate need for him.

And tonight, on the night of my twenty-fifth birthday, I think I'm ready for more.

If he'd only show up, that is.

"I'd like to make a toast!" my dad shouts out over the din of people chatting and music bumping.

I immediately flush. "Dammit, Dad."

Dana laughs and pats my back. "Honey, it's tradition."

Dad loves toasts. He makes them at every birthday or family event. I, on the other hand, hate them. He always manages to embarrass me.

My sisters crowd around me as we watch Dad try to gain the attention of the crowd, though he's flustered.

Victoria, who is only a few feet from him, sticks her fingers between her lips and whistles. "Hey! Attention, people!"

Of course she's able to hypnotize an entire room with her beauty. That settles the crowd down quick.

Dad flushes. "Thank you, Victoria." He clears his throat and then begins. "Thank you all for coming tonight to cele- brate the twenty-fifth birthday of my youngest, Amy."

If it weren't for my sisters holding me up by the elbows, I'd sink into the earth from embarrassment. Don't know why I don't mind having a crowd of kids listen to me read- ing, but when it comes to adults looking at me, I'm flustered.

"Well, I'll make it short and sweet so we can all get back

to celebrating," Dad says. "Amy, I remember the day you were born —"

"—Like it was yesterday," my sisters all say in unison.

Dad looks surprised as if we don't do this every frickin' time. "I got to start coming up with new speeches, huh?"

Dana squeezes me tighter.

"We had decided that you'd be a surprise. Didn't know if you were a girl or a boy. And after four girls, I was convinced you would be a boy. We were going to name you Theodore if you were."

"Ewww, Theo," Harley groans. I pinch her arm and she laughs.

As Dad unwinds the story of the day I was born in front of all these people, I find my gaze drifting over to the open gate at the end of the yard, hoping Hunter and Jessica will walk through at any moment. What's the hold up? Why aren't they here?

"And of course when the doctor said you were a girl, I just started laughing and said, 'Of course, she is!'" Dad's big smile falters. "Your mother asked if I was upset, but I was relieved. I didn't know what I'd do with a boy."

He has to tell the story the way it actually happened. It just sucks that my mom is implicitly involved in it. It only makes me want this to be over even sooner.

"But the truth was, my four girls would not have been complete without the fifth. The littlest. The storyteller. The lion with the gentle roar."

I smile to myself. I'm the Leo of the group. And we live in California. Doesn't matter who you are, you know astrology if you're in Cali.

"A quarter of a century...jeez, I'm getting old," Dad muses.

My sisters and I laugh. And in this moment of distraction, I see movement at the gate out of the corner of my eye.

I immediately know who it is.

Hunter walks through as subtly as he can for being nearly six and a half feet tall. In one of his hands is a gift wrapped in purple zigzag patterned paper. In the other, is Jessica's hand. She's doing a better job than him of being covert, tiptoeing carefully into the yard.

"Happy birthday, Ames," Dad announces, holding up his cocktail created signature by Harley and Kira, called Petunia's Paloma, which is just like a normal paloma with tequila, lime, and grapefruit, except it's made with lavender and has a purple hue to it, which happens to be mine and Petunia's favorite color (what can I say, I write what I know). "Cheers!"

Everyone exclaims in response, clinking their glasses and drinking. I smile and nod, thanking people, and then quickly slip out of my sisters' grasps to meet Hunter. I don't care if we're still trying to maintain a low profile. I've been waiting for him all night.

The party gets back into full swing, food and drinks flowing, music pumping.

As soon as Jessica lays eyes on me, she runs in my direction. "Happy birthday, Amy!"

I don't expect nearly as intense of a hug as I get. Jessica practically leaps straight into my arms. I'm able to catch her with a big, "Oof!" but as soon as she's there, I feel so at peace. Her little heart beating next to mine is surprisingly comforting. I know mothers feels that with their own babies. But Jessica isn't *mine*. So, why do I feel so connected to her?

"Oh, what a great hug! Thank you, sweetheart."

Hunter waits patiently for Jessica to finish her hug. He glances around nervously, not wanting to make too much of a scene. Especially not in front of my father, I'm sure.

"We brought you a present!" Jessica announces. It's clear she's not going to let go, her legs locked around my waist. Luckily, she's not too heavy. She can stay on my hip as long as she likes.

"Oh, thank you."

"Open it, open it!"

"Her hands are a little preoccupied, Jess. Come down and then she can open it," Hunter instructs calmly.

Jessica pouts but slithers down my side, planting her feet on the ground. For the first time tonight, there's no barrier between Hunter and me. The air between us is charged, pulsing with potential. My heart pounds as he takes a step toward me. The only birthday present I really want is a kiss from him. Okay, fine, I want more than a kiss. I want to wrap my body around that man like a koala on a tree and never let go. I want to have my first time and I want it with him.

But...that will take time. We can't be too obvious.

"Happy birthday, Amy," he says, holding out the gift to me.

I take it carefully and make sure my fingers brush his as I do. I want him to feel me just as much as I want to feel him. "Thank you. But you didn't have to."

"Of course we did."

I start to peel the paper carefully.

"I'll do it!" Jessica announces, reaching for the gift.

"Jess, it's Amy's present, she wants to –"

I laugh and give her the gift. "It's okay. She'll do a better job of opening it anyway. I'm always too careful."

Hunter smiles at me gratefully and we both watch as Jessica tears the wrapping paper off the box. It doesn't reveal much, just a brown gift box.

"Okay, you can open it now," Jessica says with an excited look at her dad.

I glance between them, taking the box back. I open it, revealing white tissue paper. I undo the first layer and find a small stuffed lion with big googly eyes and a bright orange mane. "A lion!" I exclaim. "I love lions."

"Daddy said you're a Leo and that's a lion," Jessica said. "I picked it out."

See? Everyone in California knows astrology. Even Hunter Ricks.

"There's more, there's more!"

"I know, I can feel it. It's kind of heavy..." I undo the rest of the tissue, my fingers brushing up against a cool layer of glass. "Oh my word..."

Colors flash before my eyes. I need to make sense of what I'm seeing at first but when I do...I feel tears in my eyes.

In a lilac colored frame is a version of the cover of *Petunia's Parental Predicament* done entirely in crayon. The title and the words are written to the best of their ability although the 'd' is backwards and some of the e's are capitalized.

"I did it," Jessica says.

In the bottom corner, Jessica has scrawled her name in big red letters. I touch it softly. "I can see that, Jess. It's beautiful."

"She insisted on doing it...it's her favorite book, so..." Hunter explains.

My eyes flick from him to Jessica and back again. I feel as though I might cry if I'm not careful. "It's beautiful. Really, really..." I shake off the weepiness. "Can I have another hug?"

Jessica grins and nods eagerly.

I hand the gift back to Hunter and wrap my arms around Jessica again. She pushes her head right into the crook of my neck. "Thank you, sweetheart."

"You're welcome!" she says in a sing-song voice.

Then, I look up at Hunter. "Thank you," I repeat.

"All I did was frame it," he says almost bashfully as if this wasn't one of the sweetest gestures. "I was going to get you something else, but, I –"

"It's perfect. Really." I pull away from Jess and push her hair out of her face. "Really."

"Jessie!" The rip roaring cry of Stella interrupts the moment. My niece comes sprinting over and grabs Jessica's hand. "We're going up to the treehouse! Can Jessica come?" Stella asks Hunter, standing on her tiptoes as if that could somehow eliminate the distance between them.

Hunter grins. "Of course."

Jessica and Stella run off down the yard in the direction of the path to the treehouse. For a brief moment I think about how easily Jessica and Hunter would fit into my family. They're already so entangled.

Getting ahead of yourself, Amy.

Probably should deal with the virginity thing first.

"If there weren't so many people around, I'd give you a birthday kiss too," Hunter murmurs.

My mouth falls ajar. The two feet between us might as well be miles now that he's said that. "Y-yeah, that could be awkward if you did."

Hunter's lips curl to the side in a knowing smile. "I'm going to grab a drink."

"Yes, of course. Please, enjoy yourself."

"And you..." He glances over my shoulder. "Should probably attend to your circle of sisters over there."

I look in the same direction. All my sisters are doing a

bad job of pretending they're not looking over at Hunter and me. I knew I'd have to answer for it sometime. Might as well be now, I guess.

"Oh god," I say, flushing.

"Guess I didn't need to kiss you for people to become suspicious," Hunter says and then walks past me in the direction of the refreshments. "Talk later, Amy."

The way he says my name sends a shiver down my spine, affirming just how much I need him.

In order to avoid watching Hunter saunter off and his cute butt as he goes, I readjust my sundress and head over to my sisters.

"Well, that looked like an interesting conversation," Harley says with a half-smile to Gillian.

"Have something to tell us?" Gillian adds; from the look on her face, she already knows what's going on. I wonder if Hunter's been talking to Axel about me. I should have known things would have been heard through the grapevine.

"Guys, come on, give her a break," Dana comes to my defense, standing up straighter beside me.

But what's the point. I know what I want and it's Hunter. And I'm sure that he wants me too. After all, he was tempted to give me a birthday kiss. I'm almost certain if I had said he could, he would have. Even amidst all these people. "It's okay, Dana. Um..." I scan the faces of my sisters, all of them eager and lovely with hope in their eyes. "Hunter and I are sort of dating."

"I knew it, I *knew* it," Kira says, balling her hands into fists. "I told you, didn't I?"

"You did," Dana says with a nod and then grabs my shoulder. "You two look cute together."

"Okay, well, you need to tell us everything," Harley

says. "I've been dying to know ever since Grant told me you two were –" She smacks her hand against her mouth.

Gillian glares. "We weren't going to say we knew."

"Don't act like it wasn't obvious!" I laugh. "Come on, let's go sit and I'll tell you everything."

My sisters and I sit poolside and I give them a play by play of what's happened between Hunter and me, a few things left out including our first indulgence poolside in his yard and the warm feelings of need growing in my pelvis. I keep it light, keep it sweet. That's what they would expect from me anyway.

Eventually, Harley splinters off to take Tana from Grant and Dana is dragged into dancing with Drew (if she says they're just friends *one* more time...). Gillian has to deal with a hungry Stella and Kira gets wrapped up in checking her work notifications while muttering under her breath how much she hates *Orlie*. Still can't get over that name.

I lean back, letting the warm night wrap itself around me and bask in the starlight pricking through the night sky. I scan the party, looking for Hunter. Just a glimpse will be enough for a bit.

However, when I see him standing and talking with my dad my blood runs cold. They're off near the willow tree speaking in what looks like serious, hushed whispers.

Relax, Amy. They could be talking about anything. It's most likely not about you.

When Dad looks up, eyes meeting mine for only a millisecond, I just know it's *definitely* about me.

My heart thumps in my chest.

Dad knows. I just *know* it. And that could quite possibly mean that my fairytale love affair ends tonight.

14

HUNTER

"I UNDERSTAND IT'S A TENDER THING," I SAY.

Kent's brow has been furrowed since the moment Amy's name came out of my mouth. I'm only glad that when I continued on to say, "have been seeing one another," his nostrils didn't start to flare.

"I would have said something sooner, but we have been taking things so slow and...you know, didn't want to air all of her business out to you, being her father. But I also know we're friends."

Kent clears his throat and nods. "We are."

Not "we were"...that's a good sign.

"And given how my feelings are developing for her, I want to bring it to your attention and ask for your blessing to continue seeing her and allow things to get more serious. Perhaps."

Kent rubs his chin and glances off in the direction of the party. My eyes have been firmly locked on him the whole time. Nothing else can distract me from my mission. "Listen, Hunter..."

My heart braces for impact. If he doesn't give his permission, I have no choice but to respect his wishes. But, god, it will rip me apart. Will rip Jessica apart too. And I'm not sure how I'll handle that, so I just put on a brave face and start planning my exit route just in case.

"You know, if I've learned anything in the past couple years, is that my girls are grown. They're adults." Kent swallows and then locks eyes with me. "They make their own decisions. And if you want to pursue Amy, then the only opinion that matters is hers."

I breathe a sigh of relief.

"As long as she's happy – and you're respectful, Hunter. I know your habits for –"

"Promise, Kent, what I'm feeling for Amy is nothing like that. Not at all."

Kent's brow finally releases and he smiles. In silence, he reaches his hand out to me to shake. I accept it, filled with gratitude when I feel the intensity of his grip.

"Thank you," I whisper.

"Don't thank me yet," Kent says, looking askance. "You've got someone else to answer to for your feelings."

I finally loosen my gaze from him and look toward the party. My eyes immediately land on Amy who is cautiously idling on the outskirts of the festivities, pretending like she's not looking at us. All that relief immediately goes away. *Fuck, I have to tell her how I feel.*

The feelings I'm having...they're serious. They're not love. Not yet. That would scare her off. And given that we haven't consummated our relationship in the bedroom, I wouldn't dare throw that word around for fear that she might feel pressured to give herself over to me. I'll wait as long as she needs.

Amy does make it very difficult, though. Just seeing this pretty green and yellow dress draped over her torso and her nipples poking out through the fabric makes me want to –

"Okay, I don't know what you're thinking, but I don't like it," Kent says with a groan.

I shake my head. "I'm not –" I start to lie even though I very much was thinking about ripping Amy's dress off.

"Best of luck," Kent says and pats my back, a meek chuckle on his lips. Then, he walks off toward the drink table where Victoria, Grant's sister, waits for him with a stiff drink. For a famous model, someone who is looked at all the time, she certainly has an uncanny ability for reading a room.

Amy doesn't waste a single moment making her way over to me. I like that she really says, "fuck being subtle". It's both charming and refreshing. "What was that about?"

"Hello to you too."

"Why were you talking to my dad?" She crosses her arms over her chest.

I tilt my head to the side and smile. "You're worried."

"Of course I'm worried! You two were talking over here like it's Fort Knox or something, and when Dad looked right at me, well, I just knew –"

"Hey, hey, hey, relax, honey," I say and gently touch her forearm. "It's okay. I promise, everything's okay."

We both look at the point of contact, my fingers lingering on her arm. I withdraw them cautiously for her sake more than mine. "I told him about us."

Her eyes flash with fire. "You what?!"

"I just wanted to get his permission. To continue seeing you. Since it feels like things are getting more serious."

Amy's anger abates. "Oh."

I chew on the inside of my lip. "Am I wrong?"

"N-no! No, of course not," Amy says adamantly.

"Good."

There is a hush under the tree. Despite the party bumping and bubbling around us, I can only hear the leaves shuffling together. Conjuring something.

"I know how hard things were once he found out about Grant and Harley...in fact, Grant suggested I let him know about us before it got too intense so it didn't blindside him."

"In case I get pregnant out of wedlock, huh?" Amy says wryly.

I don't even know how to respond to that because all the horny cells in my brain start screaming. The thought of getting Amy in bed is one thing. The thought of having a baby with her is another. Equally stirring.

"Bad joke, sorry," Amy squeaks.

"No, no, just..." I take a deep breath. "You're so beautiful. It makes me lose my place sometimes."

Amy's lips curl into her signature warm smile. "Oh, gosh."

"Really, it's staggering sometimes."

Another hush.

"What...what did my dad say?" Amy asks carefully.

"Oh, right. *That*."

"Yeah, *that*."

We both laugh lightly. She makes me feel like a schoolboy trying to talk to a girl at her locker between passing periods. Terrified, needy, flushed.

Totally infatuated with her.

"He basically said that the only opinion that matters is yours," I say.

Amy's eyebrows lift. "Really?"

I nod.

"Well, that's a far cry from the father who clocked Grant in the face when he found out he was Harley's baby daddy."

"Listen, I'm a girl dad. I can understand the impulse," I reply.

Amy laughs and then, with her eye toward the party, takes a tiny step toward me. "So, it's up to me, is it?"

"Seems so."

She tilts her head back; her lips are painted in a raspberry hue. I'd love to taste them. "Well, you have my permission to get more serious with me."

Her voice...there's a quality to it I've never heard. Deeper. Suggestive.

Maybe it's just my imagination. My stupid, horned up brain dreaming about burying myself inside her.

But then her fingers touch the back of my hand and then loop through mine own. "Because I want to get more serious with you."

Don't get hard. Do NOT get hard.

"Hunter?"

"What?" I ask so softly I'm not even sure I spoke.

Another step toward me. Lips at the ready.

Everyone knows now. There is no use hiding it.

I start to lean forward to plant my lips against hers. A sealing of our seriousness. A hope for more. Soon.

But before I can even get that first tender kiss, I hear a familiar cry. "Daaaaaddy..."

I snap out of my hazy, Amy-filled hypnosis and see Jessica standing in the yard looking for me, her whole body droopy. "Jess! Over here!" I wave to get her attention.

Jessica zeroes in on me and toddles over in our direction.

To my disappointment, Amy steps away from me to make room for the other woman in my life.

"Daddy, I'm tired," Jessica mumbles, reaching her arms up for me.

"You are? But we just got here, sweet pea," I say, trying to veil my disappointment as I lift her up into my arms. "Don't you want to stay a bit longer and celebrate Amy's big day with her?"

Jessica shakes her head, letting it rest against my clavicle with a thud.

I rub her back. "We haven't even had cake yet..." I'm not usually the type to push her past her limits. Jessica's well-being comes first always. However, Amy and I were just about to cross an important threshold and I don't want to abandon her just yet.

"It's okay," Amy murmurs and touches my arm. She looks at Jessica lovingly. "I'll save some just for you."

Jessica reaches her hand out to Amy. "Promise?"

Amy takes it and kisses the back of it. "Promise."

I sigh. "Sorry, Amy, I –"

"Really, Hunter, it's okay. I promise, it's alright."

I'm devastated when her hand slides down my arm and she steps away. "I'll see you. Soon."

My lips burn with want for her. *Come back. Kiss me goodbye.* "As soon as possible."

Amy smiles, nods, and then walks away.

Being a parent has many inconveniences. And while I'd never blame Jessica for her needs as a little one trying to navigate this big world, it's hard not to feel miserable as I walk through the gate, leaving behind the loud Solace yard for the quiet of mine.

Just me and Jessica. That's how it's been for almost three whole years.

However, it won't be that forever. Not anymore. Not now that Amy is in our lives.

One day, we'll walk into the quiet of my home together, tuck Jessica into bed, and retire to our bed where we will worship one another until the end of time.

I just know it.

15

———

AMY

THE PAPER PLATE BENDS UNDER THE WEIGHT OF THE rich, frosting filled cake as I walk through the darkened yard.

It's much past midnight already. But I couldn't sleep.

Since the moment he left the party, the only thing on my mind has been Hunter.

I arrive at the gate and stare at it. This seems like the hardest part, walking through this godforsaken gate. I still don't know why my anxiety trembles when I look at it or why my heart pulses with the fierceness of a wild horse. However, I have to face it.

Because on the other side...is my future.

My destiny.

I gently press the latch and push the gate open. Hunter's yard is equally dark, but his pool is closer to the house and lights up the siding.

I did it. I'm here.

However, now is the trial of actually getting *inside*. I can't ring the doorbell or knock on the door without the fear of waking up Jessica and I can't just waltz inside. I doubt he'd leave a door unlocked and, if he did, I'm sure there are some alarms that are engaged.

I walk further into the yard and up the steps of the deck, staring through the darkened sliding glass doors.

I didn't think this far ahead. I touch the pocket of my robe. Empty. I stupidly left my phone in the kitchen when I was loading the cake onto the plate.

Shows you how much of an idiot you can be when you're horny.

Maybe this was a mistake. Maybe I should have texted him ahead of time or just be a good girl and wait until a more appropriate moment.

But I'm *so tired* of being a good girl.

Just try. Just see. What's the worst that can happen?

Probably a lot of things. However, my heart is beating for Hunter. He's the only thing on my mind.

I touch the handle of the sliding glass door and pull. Miraculously, it slides open. *Yes.*

I step into the living room of the Ricks house, totally dark except for a small aquarium bubbling in the corner with Jessica's beta fish, Brody, swishing around.

Through the hallway, I can see there's a light on in the front of the house. One lamp casting a warm glow into the room.

I tiptoe through the house. Past the downstairs bathroom, the door to the kitchen, and into the foyer. The light is coming from the sitting room in the front, a modern looking lamp hanging over an easy chair where there's a book folded over the arm of the chair, in the midst of being read.

"Amy."

I stifle a cry and turn around to find Hunter standing in the foyer behind me, confusion all over his face.

"What are you doing here?"

I don't have words to speak. He takes them all out of my mouth with his beauty. I've never seen him in his night-clothes, an old T-shirt and boxers, but damn is it a good look on him. His long locks hang wild and free over his shoulders.

And his eyes...

Warm, amber, inviting.

"Amy? You okay?"

"Cake."

Hunter's eyebrows jump and he half-smiles. "What?"

"I – I – I brought cake for Jessica. Here," I say, holding the plate out.

Hunter starts to walk toward me, slowly, purposefully. I feel my heartbeat in my groin. He inclines his head to the side. "You let yourself into my home in the middle of the night to bring cake for my daughter?"

I nod. "Uh-huh. I mean, I know it seems ridiculous, but..."

Hunter stops a foot away from me. "Doesn't seem ridiculous to me."

I feel like I'm breathing so heavily and nothing has even happened yet. Can he hear me panting already?

Hunter's lower lip curls under his teeth. I'd like to feel him nibble all over my body. My neck, my breasts, the insides of my thighs.

I'm turning into someone I don't recognize.

But I like her. I'd like her to stay.

"Well, I'll take it and then –" Hunter begins to hold his hand out for the plate.

I can't take it anymore. I drop the plate to the ground and close the space between us, bounding into Hunter's arms and kissing him with all my might.

Hunter gasps, but Immediately wraps his arms around me.

As I kiss him, let my tongue roll into his mouth, I pull my legs up around his waist. His hands slide down to my waist, teetering toward my backside nervously.

Let me be clearer.

I tear my lips from his and murmur, "I want you."

"Oh god," he replies.

I toy with the locks of his hair at the base of his skull and graze the tip of my nose against his cheek. "I want you to be my first."

Hunter's hands tentatively sneak around my ass cheeks. He squeezes them. "Are you sure?"

"Mhm."

"We don't need to rush, Amy."

"I know."

"I'll wait, I'll wait as long as you –"

"Hunter."

He stops speaking, mouth hung open, his perfect lips sheened from our kiss.

"Tonight. I want you tonight. *Now*."

Hunter's hands tighten needily around my ass; he kisses me again, a low grunt in the back of his throat reverberating into my mouth. "You're sure?" he asks once more.

I press my forehead to his. "I've never been surer of anything in my life." For the first time in my life, I'm following what my gut tells me to do. Hunter brings it out of me. Every cell in my body knows that he's right for me. I have no reservations.

"Then hold on, baby," Hunter says with a cocked smile.

I don't have time to respond before Hunter is barreling up the stairs to the second floor. I laugh into his neck, trying not to make too much noise since Jessica is just down the hall.

Before I know it, we're in Hunter's bedroom. I've never seen the inside of it. And as soon as Hunter throws me down on the bed, I know I'm not going to. At least not tonight.

Hunter undoes the tie closure on my robe and opens it wide, revealing my light cotton nightgown. It's the closest thing I have to something "sexy" unless I came out in just underwear. And that's not me. I'd much rather look like a Victorian heroine when I'm losing my virginity.

Hunter grabs the hem of my nightgown and starts to push it up my legs. "I want you to feel amazing tonight, Amy."

My breath halts in my chest.

He stops right before he reveals my most sensitive parts. His warm, broad hand settles on my thigh. "You tell me at any point to stop and I'll stop. Always...*always*."

I smile. "Don't stop yet."

Hunter laughs and sinks to his knees before the bed. "You have no idea how badly I've wanted this."

"Me too."

He smiles a genuine smile. Not suave, not charismatic. *Real.* Hunter pushes the nightgown the rest of the way up, exposing my groin and belly. He touches my stomach, fingers trailing down to the waistband of my underwear.

This is it.

"Oh, Amy..." he mutters, sinking to his knees before the bed and starting to pull the underwear down.

I prop myself up on my elbows to watch him as he removes my panties. He tosses them to the side and then kisses the inside of my ankle. Then my calf...then my knee...

"W-what are you doing?" I ask.

Hunter stops, lifting his head just before he can plant a kiss to my thigh. "I'm going to taste you."

I stare at him like he's just spoken gibberish.

"Is that alright?"

I blink.

"Has no one ever tasted you before, Amy?"

I shake my head.

Hunter's eyes are firmly in mine as he kisses the inside of my thigh. His beard tickles and bristles my skin. Higher and higher until I can feel his breath on my vulva. "I won't do it if you don't want me to. But..." He turns his head to the inside of my other thigh and kisses it. *God*, how he's teasing me. My clit is throbbing for him, almost like I'm in pain. "I think it will help loosen you up." His hand slides under my thigh, down my leg to my ankle. He props it up on his shoulder.

Hunter looks fucking amazing between my legs like this.

"Should I stop?"

"*No*," I answer with an adamance I didn't know I felt. "Do it."

"Thank god," Hunter says and repositions his mouth over my pussy. "If you would have said no, I would have been..." He takes a deep inhale of my scent and shakes his head with reverence. "So disappointed."

Without another word, he carefully slides his tongue between the lips of my vagina. My stomach muscles seize.

"Mm...tastes even better than I could have imagined, Amy," he says and then presses his lips flush with my lower ones.

Watching Hunter devour me is unlike anything I have ever imagined. I've never allowed a man this close to me. In my fantasies, I always thought it would just be a classic missionary position. Something quick and easy. To get that first time out of the way.

But Hunter is determined to make this the best first time in the history of mankind.

"Lay back," he mutters quickly, his hand sliding up my belly to my chest. "Relax."

I follow his instructions and *give in*. I close my eyes, letting the feelings wash over me. The pressure his mouth puts on my swollen lips is exquisite; from time to time, he swirls his tongue around my clit causing my whole body to jerk, my pubic bone ramming into his nose.

Hunter likes that; I can tell from the way he chuckles into me. Just more stimulus, more vibrations causing swirling sensations of warm pleasure through my belly.

"Oh god, Hunter..." I moan and run my hands through the skeins of his hair.

Hunter responds by hooking his arms around my legs and pushing my hips back so they're slightly raised off the bed, his mouth works harder and more voraciously.

It's so warm. His bedroom might as well be Death Valley, otherwise I've come down with a fever. It's so intense it scares me. My hips start to ride against his mouth, out of my control. My clit needs it, but with every pulse I feel hotter. I'm burning up. "Mm. You can't – you can't –" I balk.

He tears his lips away from me. "I'm stopping, I'm stopping."

I try to catch my breath. Why do I feel like crying?

Hunter slides up the bed beside me, his hand resting on my stomach. "Hey, it's okay. Too intense?"

I nod. "Y-yeah."

He touches my cheek softly. "It's just me, baby. It's just me."

I look at him, though my heart beats with terror.

"Did it feel good?"

"Yes. I just got really hot."

He smiles. "That happens."

"I think I need to take this off..." I say, sitting up and pulling at my nightgown.

"Let me help you."

We jointly wriggle the nightgown off my body, leaving my breasts exposed to the air. Hunter doesn't make a move for them, which I'm grateful for. I do feel his eyes on them. *That* I like. "Your turn," I say and grab onto his shirt.

Hunter grins. "Only fair."

I wave his hands off as he tries to pull the shirt off. I work it up his body methodically, revealing his impeccable muscles bit by bit. Hunter lifts his arms for me to pull the shirt off; I toss it aside. "Mm...you're perfect," I say, running my hand down his hairy, washboard abs.

"So are you."

I flush and press an arm over my breasts as if he hasn't just seen my whole naked body.

Hunter leans over to me and kisses my shoulder. "We can stop any time, Amy. Right now, if you like."

"I don't want to stop," I say firmly. "I want to keep going."

Hunter nods. "Okay."

I tentatively kiss him; I can taste the tang of what must be my juices on his lips and in his beard.

Hunter takes my hand. "Do you want to touch me?"

More terror. But the excited kind. "Yes."

Measuredly, Hunter places my hand on the inside of his knee and guides it upward bit by bit. When I hit the fabric of his boxers, I gasp.

Hunter laughs. "Almost, Amy. Almost."

A bit farther and then...I feel the lump in his shorts. I widen my hand and grab onto it, unsure how much pressure to use.

He inhales slightly. "You don't have to be too gentle."

I grab a bit harder, massaging it back and forth in my hand.

"Jesus Christ," he says and then laughs.

"What, am I –"

"It's perfect, it's perfect, I just..." Hunter shakes his head. "All you've done is touch me and I feel like coming."

My heart pounds. To have that kind of power over him...well, I can hardly believe it. I get a little braver and sneak my hand through the waistband of his boxers and grab him bare in my hand.

"Shit, okay –"

Something about it is intuitive. Like my hand was meant to wrap around his cock, fingers meant to tease the soft, malleable pocket of his testicles.

"You sure you haven't done this before?" Hunter asks, trying to remain humorous, but fading faster than he'd like.

"Do you have a condom?" I ask in response.

I've never seen him move so fast; Hunter rolls off the side of the bed and rips the drawer of his nightstand open. From inside, he pulls out a golden wrapped condom. Hunter pushes his boxers down to the floor, revealing his thick, long cock.

How all that is going to fit inside me, I don't know, but I'm looking forward to trying.

"Can I put it on you?" I ask.

Hunter shakes his head and climbs back onto the bed, kneeling before me. "You're full of surprises. Here."

I unwrap the condom; I remember putting one on a

banana back in sex ed. But this is the real deal and I've decided a dick is really not like a banana at all.

Hunter holds his penis at the base so it's straight up for me.

I place the condom on the tip and begin to roll it down.

"Good – nngh – girl." His throat grips at the words as my fingers slide down his shaft.

Once it's on, I lean back on my hands before him. My confidence is gaining. I want him to see all of me.

"Are you...are you ready, honey?" Hunter asks, carefully placing one of his hands next to my hip.

I lay back into the pillows of the king bed and spread my legs for him to nestle between. "Yes, I'm ready."

Hunter doesn't reply with words. Instead, he kisses me softly on the lips, his body closing in on mine. I can feel his hard cock leaning up against my groin.

I can't believe this is really happening.

Hunter shifts his hips back and forth, sliding his length through my folds, preparing me. "Just breathe, alright? It won't hurt if you breathe."

"Sounds like you've done this before," I say, only half-joking.

He kisses my forehead. "This is the only time that matters. Here with you."

It doesn't matter how many women he's had or how many times he's had sex. Hunter is making my first time... perfect so far. I wrap my arms around his neck and draw him into a longing kiss. "Okay, I'm ready," I whisper.

Hunter reaches his hand in between our bodies, adjusts his cock, and suddenly, the tip is inside. Just pops in like nothing.

"Keep going."

"Slow and steady, Ames."

Hunter presses his length bit by bit inside me with tiny thrusts of his hips. It does hurt at first, the stretch of something inside me that's never been there before. But with each deepening, Hunter distracts me with a kiss or a caress.

Without me realizing, my hips have started to work with him, rolling back to accept him deeper and deeper inside me.

"Is it okay?"

"Feels good," I say. The stretching has turned from pain to pleasure.

Hunter purses his lips, rolling his hips a little faster. His eyes are locked in mine. Focused. Looking for any reason he should stop.

I'm not going to give it to him, though. My body accepts him, sparks with heat as he rubs up against parts of me that have never been touched by a man.

And in no time flat, it's happening. It's really happening. This thing I imagined for years and years that seemed almost impossible.

I'd almost begun to believe I'd be a virgin until the day I died if I didn't give it up to whatever John, Dick, or Harry walked through my life.

But I waited.

And thank god I did because this, here with Hunter, is... incredible. Our hips interlocking, our bodies pulsing together like we've choreographed it. Like we've done it a thousand times.

Faster and faster, I feel it building in my pelvis. The heat again...better this time.

"Oh, Amy, you feel so good."

I whimper in response, locking my ankles around his hips.

Hunter curses as I trap him deep inside me. Suddenly,

he pushes himself back onto his knees, taking me with him so my lower back is off the bed. "God, you look amazing."

With every thrust, my breasts bounce and my heart flutters in a way I've never felt. I didn't know the feelings were full body, but here I am.

"Tell me how you feel," he says breathlessly.

"Good," I say, grabbing onto the pillows as if they'll help me maintain composure.

"Look me in the eye and tell me how you feel."

I turn to look at Hunter, immediately captivated by his hot, fiery stare. Just as I wrap my mouth around the words, "So good," he slides his thumb against my clitoris. I gasp, pressing a pillow up to my mouth and moaning.

Hunter's eyes are locked in mine. His thumb circles my clit. "I'm going to make you come, Amy."

I moan again.

His hips move faster. The heat. It's back. This time, I know that I'm supposed to let myself get overwhelmed by it. Tears of pleasure prick my eyes.

"Say my name." His chest rumbles against mine.

"Hunter…" I say, digging my fingernails into his back. "Hunter, please. *Please.*"

Each of his thrusts comes with ragged breath.

I gasp for air, nearly suffocating myself, holding my body tighter and tighter until at once all the tension releases. I scream despite myself, burying my face in his neck to muffle the sound. I tremble in his arms as quivering pleasure rolls through my body. Again, again. My entire body goes limp like a snapped rubber band.

Then, Hunter sputters in my ear, gripping the pillows. He shoves himself deep inside me once more and curses. I feel him coming, his member tensing inside me. With a heavy sigh, he collapses on top of me, curling me into his arms. He peppers kisses to the side of my face and my neck. "How did you feel?" he asks, dry-mouthed and yet still determined to sound like he's in control.

The tears in my eyes start to fall. "So good."

He doesn't question them, just wipes them away.

I know there's no place I'd rather be than right here with him.

"YOU'LL STAY FOR BREAKFAST, won't you?" Hunter asks the moment our eyes meet the next morning.

How the hell am I going to refuse that?

And I'm glad that I don't. There's a quality to waking up next to someone. The intimacy...feels different. Both lazier and more purposeful at once. We chose to sleep beside one another, entangled in limbs, vulnerable and naked.

Now, we just get to appreciate each other's presence without any sort of posturing.

Well, except when it comes to Jessica.

We both get dressed and head down into the kitchen. "Waffles or French toast?" he asks me. And I just gape at him. He's a perfect man.

"French toast it is," he says with a wink.

I watch as he grabs a loaf of bread out of the pantry and then the eggs from the fridge. He sets them down on the counter and gets to work, his back to me. I like it when he's not looking at me. Then I get to stare at him as much as I want.

I go up behind him and wrap my arms around his chest, burying my face in his back. Deep breath...his pheromones are incredible.

Hunter touches my hand. "Hey."

"Hey," I reply and kiss his spine.

"Why is there cake on the floor?!"

Hunter and I snap apart at the sound of Jessica's tinkling voice from the foyer. I blanch; we forgot to clean up the fucking cake.

Hunter rushes to meet her in the foyer. "Amy brought it for you from the party, but Daddy was sort of a klutz and dropped it," I hear him explain.

I giggle to myself.

"Come with me. I have a surprise for you," he adds.

I wait in the kitchen, my heart pounding. When he rounds the corner with Jess, her face breaks into a smile. "Amy! You came for breakfast!"

I hold back a laugh. *Yes, "came for breakfast" is an apt description.*

Jessica squirms in Hunter's arms, reaching for me. I meet his gaze quickly for permission, but he doesn't hesitate to bring her over to me. I engulf her in an early morning hug, her dark brown bedhead tickling my cheeks. "How'd you sleep?" I ask tenderly.

She nestles into me. "Will you bring me more cake?"

Hunter and I both laugh. "Yes, but first, breakfast. French toast. How does that sound?"

Jessica lifts her head with a big smile. "Mmm!"

"You girls sit back and relax. I'll get breakfast done in no time," Hunter says in a gruff morning voice that sends a shiver down my spine.

"Yes, Daddy," Jessica says.

I'm inclined to echo her sentiment but hold my tongue.

The two of us sit at the kitchen table and play "I Spy" until breakfast is ready. When Hunter sets the plates of French toast decorated with powdered sugar and berries, I feel like I'm at brunch or something. "This looks...amazing."

It tastes amazing too. "Where did you learn to cook like this?" I ask before I've finished chewing.

"Swallow before you speak, Amy," Jessica reminds me.

I flush and Hunter laughs. "Well, when I was a kid, I spent a lot of time with our house staff. I know that sounds very...grandiose, but –"

"It's where you came from. I want to hear all about it."

Hunter smiles gratefully. "Yes, well, Brigitte was our chef. And she always invited me into the kitchen to help her with the cooking. I just fell in love with it. In fact, before I took over the Ricks Group, I had been traveling a lot to try different cuisines and...I don't know, eventually open a restaurant of my own."

"Hunter, that's amazing," I say. "Can't you picture it, Jess? Daddy in a white jacket and a chef's hat."

Jessica's lips sour. "That would look silly."

We both laugh. Hunter waves his hand. "Listen, it was a pipe dream."

I reach out and touch his arm across the table. "If that's what you want to do, you should do it. You have the resources –"

"But I don't have the *time*," Hunter replies. "Between work and..." He hesitates to say Jessica's name, but the way his eyes flick to her says enough.

I hold back what I want to say next. *If we were together, you'd have more time. I could take care of Jessica too. We could follow our dreams together.*

"Amy?" Jessica suddenly peeps.

"Yes, honey. Do you need me to cut more of your French toast?"

She pats her mouth with her napkin delicately as if she's

seen it done that way many times before. "Are you my mommy now?"

The room goes silent. Thankfully, Jessica doesn't notice Hunter and me sweating.

"Um..." I begin, looking to Hunter.

"Well, Jessica, it's a bit more complicated than –"

The doorbell rings. *Saved by the bell, literally.* I immediately jump to my feet. "I'll get it!"

If Hunter asks me to wait, I don't hear him. I need to get out of the room.

Jessica's question terrified me. It's not that I don't feel capable of being her mother. If the connection between Hunter and me continues to grow the way it has, I don't see any reason I wouldn't be able to step into the role full-heartedly.

That's what actually scares me. That I'm not afraid of it.

That I *want* it.

I shake the thoughts away once I reach the front door, readjust my robe, and pull open the door.

I'm greeted by a tall, gaunt woman with dark hair and piercing green eyes. The moment she sees me, her neutral expression falters into a sneer. "Who are you?"

"I'm –" Isn't that what I'm supposed to be asking *her?*

The woman takes a step forward over the threshold, propelling me back into the foyer. "What are you doing in *my home?*"

"I don't u-understand. This isn't –" I've never seen this woman in my life. Is this one of the girls Hunter used to putz around with? Feeling scorned and needing to confront him?

"Veronica."

I turn to look at Hunter. He's standing in the doorway

of the kitchen, filling up the whole frame with his stature. Jessica tries to hide behind his leg, peeking out delicately.

"What...what are you doing here?"

Veronica beams and pushes past me. "Oh, Hunter, don't you recognize your wife?"

My world shatters in an instant.

16

HUNTER

"You've got some fucking balls, Veronica," I say tersely as I pace in front of my ex-wife as she sits on the couch.

She has made herself quite at home, leaning back into the pillows as if she owns the place. "Listen, how was I supposed to know she was your neighbor? I just thought some little girl came to answer your door and needed to be put in her place."

I pinch my nose bridge. It was close to impossible explaining the situation to Amy. Mostly because I couldn't even make sense of it myself. Veronica, my ex-wife, paying us a house call out of the blue, decides to play the territorial card when she sees I'm not here alone. She doesn't want to be married to me but she also can't stand me moving on. Classic narcissist. "She's not a little girl."

Veronica raises an inky eyebrow. "Compared to me, she is."

"Well, maybe that's a good thing," I say.

"Could you stop walking back and forth? This is like Wimbledon."

I plant my feet and cross my arms over my chest. "Okay. Talk."

Veronica half-laughs. "What do you want me to say?"

"Well, for starters, what the hell are you doing here showing up without warning? How the hell am I going to explain all this to –" I stop short and ball my hands into fists. I was lucky that Jessica listened when I sent her out into the yard only moments after Veronica arrived. But she's not dumb. She knows something is up. Hopefully, she's well distracted over at the Solace house with Amy. Even though I could see the hurt on Amy's face, after hearing my quick explanation, she rushed outside to take care of Jessica.

I don't deserve that woman. I really don't.

Veronica admires her nails. They're crisply done. They didn't use to be that way. Not at the end. I admit, she looks good compared to the last time I saw her. Not in a way that I'm attracted to her. Just in a way I'm not afraid for her life anymore. "Fine. I'll just come out with it point blank." She claps her hands and folds them into her lap. "I want you back, H."

It's a stupid nickname now, but back in the day could charm the pants right off me. Literally. However, it's the rest of what she says that blows my mind. "Sorry?"

"I know it's been, what, almost three years? But..." Veronica swallows, her eyes fall to the ground. "I've done a lot of work on myself. And I've changed."

"That sounds exactly like what someone who hasn't changed would say."

She glares, her green eyes sparkling. I used to be so infatuated with those green eyes. They reminded me of everything good in the world. Leaves on trees, grass, sea water. By the end, all I saw in those eyes was money. Greenbacks piling up in her eyes as she got thinner and thinner and her heart became hollower.

I wouldn't wish addiction on my worst enemy. I wouldn't wish loving an addict on them either.

"Jessica deserves a mother, don't you think? And not whoever that *girl* is, but –"

"Amy is a grown woman. Alright? I'm not going to have you disrespecting her to me."

Veronica pauses; her eyes narrow. "Don't tell me you're actually considering…"

"I'm considering lots of things; you'll have to be more specific."

She clears her throat and doesn't dare finish what she was saying. "*Amy* is not fit to be Jessica's mother like I am."

"I beg to differ, considering everything."

"Hunter, don't be cruel."

I'll be however I want. "You walked out on her, Veronica."

"I was sick."

"You were on *blow*. That's not –"

"It *is a sickness*!" she says harshly.

I stare into her eyes. Her pupils are dilated. Just the way they always used to be when she was on cocaine. However, she isn't acting like she's on cocaine. Still, I don't trust her. Not one bit.

"So, what are you going to do? Marry her? Have her be Jessica's new mother? You're going to replace me?"

"I haven't heard from you in *years*. *Jessica* has no reason to believe you'd ever act like her mother, why should I?"

"You don't want me back, then," Veronica says sternly, reaching for her purse.

Thank god, get the fuck out of here. "No, I'm glad that's been made clear."

"Fine, then I'm suing you for custody," she announces as she stands.

I shake my head. Did she really just say what I think she did? "Sorry?"

"I'm clean now. I've been to rehab. Twice, actually. And –" She reaches into her purse and pulls out a ring. She slides it onto her left ring finger. "I'm engaged, so."

"What the fuck is going on?" I say, clutching my head. "You just wanted me back and –"

Veronica shrugs. "If I could have our family back, that's what I wanted. He knows I'm here and I had to try. For my daughter's sake."

What kind of man who would go as far as to ask a woman to marry him would allow for that? Her story not only doesn't make sense. It's suspicious beyond belief. I don't believe for a second she ever wanted me back. "Don't you dare call her your –"

"I gave birth to her. *That's what she is.*"

I would never take that away from her. She did carry Jessica, nurtured her with her body as long as she could. I pray to god she truly remained clean the whole time Jessica was in Veronica's womb. For all intents and purposes, from the way Jess turned out, it seems all signs point to yes.

"I want to be in her life. And you had the chance to have it the way you always wanted, H."

I cringe again at the nickname.

Veronica pulls her purse over her shoulder. "My lawyer will be in touch with you."

"Your lawyer..." I say with a dry laugh.

"Yes, *my lawyer.*"

When we split, she had nothing except alimony. And the prenup stipulated enough to protect me from being fleeced out of house and home. However, if she's hiring a lawyer, she's gotten the best of the best. That's the only way they can compete with my legal team.

Something tells me she's got more money than just my alimony coming in. This guy...I wonder who he is. And I wonder what kind of money he makes. And if he makes it honestly.

"It's my right as her mother to get to know her."

"And it's my right as her father and sole custodial guardian to protect her from people I see as dangerous to her young mind. You understand that, right? Since you're so keen on what's 'best' for her?" I reply.

Veronica straightens up. For once she doesn't have a sharp comeback. We were together long enough that I know all of her tells. Her cheek twitching, her eyes rolling to the side. I've scathed her.

"You didn't want to be a mother," I tell her. That's as much as she told me when she walked out only a month after Jess was born. "You said you –"

"I was all screwed up. You know that."

This whole thing was screwed up from start to finish. I met Veronica on my travels. She was just a backpacker traveling Southeast Asia and I was a billionaire looking for some company. She was gorgeous and witty; I was lonely and...I ignored all the signs we weren't meant to be. Then it was too late.

I shouldn't say that. I don't regret Jessica's birth. I don't regret being her father.

This whole time, though, I know Veronica has.

So, why is she back? Why could she possibly want a relationship with Jess now?

"I look forward to seeing you in court, then," I say and then step into the front hall. "Now if you'll excuse me..." I open the front door and gesture toward the outside.

Veronica strides slowly toward me and then glances out the door. "We could have done this amicably."

"No, you know we never could have done that." It has two meanings. The first being that things between us are broken. Irreparably so. The second...I'm not convinced she ever wanted to cooperate with me. There's a story here. And I don't know all of it. "And Veronica?"

"Hm?"

"You better not be on anything. Or near anything. Or near anyone who is on anything. Because if I get even a whiff of it, so help me god..." I don't know what the end of that sentence is. If she came near my daughter – *my daughter* – with even a speck of a contact high, I'd lose it. I'd really lose it.

Veronica's body tenses. "I told you, I'm clean."

"For some reason, I don't trust you."

She laughs in an empty way. "You used to."

I hold my tongue. I don't think I ever really did.

"Be seeing you."

Hopefully not.

I watch her leave through the door and go out to her car. A respectable blue sedan. Economy type of car. I wait until her car has pulled out of the driveway and she speeds off down the street. I wonder how she got my address. How she got in through the gate. So many questions. No answers.

I stand there for a long time looking out at my front yard. The August heat seeps into the house and the air conditioner kicks on angrily.

The ground I stand on feels unsteady. I'm standing on a Faultline, waiting for the earth to split apart and swallow me whole.

There's no way I'm going to lose Jessica. No fucking way.

And then there's Amy...what do I do about Amy? Every spare moment I've had, every wick of emotion, any *time* I've had have gone to her.

I might have to press pause.

Just pause.

But she's so young...so blessedly new to all of this.

In doing what I have to do, I might break her heart. And that's nearly as bad as losing Jessica.

Nearly.

17

______

AMY

"I promise I'm not ending things."

Hunter's words ricochet through my mind every few minutes. I can't get lost in work for too long without remembering his crestfallen expression as he explained the situation to me.

His ex, back for Jessica. I can't imagine how terrifying that is.

Actually, I can. I've known Jessica since she was a baby, but in the short time Hunter and I have been seeing each other, I've fallen desperately in love with her.

Just like I have with her father.

I wonder, if he knew that I loved Jessica like I do if he'd push me away.

Losing her would be just as bad as losing him. So, I let him take a step back from me. Even though my body feels betrayed. Just a few nights ago I was lost in his arms, feeling pleasure I had never felt. I was worshiped. I felt divine.

Now, I feel like yesterday's crumpled up newspaper. Discarded and damaged.

I feel a bit foolish for being so bereft over it. Hunter

never mentioned that we'd have to stop seeing each other or that he wouldn't be in touch. Just that it might be less... strained, even.

Still, though. It felt like we were just stepping into the next phase of our relationship. Like everything was possible.

Apparently, everything *was* possible. I just never accounted for the bad things.

In order to avoid the mere possibility of seeing Hunter (or Jessica, for that matter), I've posted up at Gillian's bakery for the day. I've spread out all my materials at a table: my sketchbook, computer, some writing materials. From time to time, my sister or Lola, her best friend and co-owner of the store, pop by with another sweet treat for me. Usually, I wouldn't indulge so much, but I'm grieving, so it seems only right.

My art reflects my mood too. Poor Petunia is getting put through it today on the page. In one sketch, she's sitting in the rain, pummeled with raindrops that are mixing with her tears. In another one, her favorite dress has been shrunk in the wash.

Art is catharsis, what can I say?

Around noon, Gillian drops into the chair beside me. "We're putting in a lunch order. What do you want?"

"Depends what we're getting."

Gillian smiles. "Vegan food."

"Wow, shocking."

"It's good, it's this vegan chicken place. You'll like it. It's like –"

"The real thing," I finish her sentence with a smile. "Sure it is."

Gillian laughs and puts her arm around the back of my chair. "It is, I promise."

"Just get me one of whatever you're having," I say, and continue shading the underside of a storm cloud.

"Jeez, Amy. Looks sad."

"Yeah, well, I feel sad."

I can feel Gillian's eyes on me, her head tilting to the side as she considers the best way to help me. I wish I was better at keeping things to myself. But the second Hunter told me we had to cool things down, I blabbered to Kira. And while Kira usually is the most locked lipped of us all, she texted all the rest of my sisters to let them know what was going on.

Now that they all know, I can feel their constant pity. Whether it's in real life or in their "checking in" text messages. Dana sent me one every hour on the hour yesterday until I sent her a few angry faced emojis and wrote, "Stop asking!"

She did stop asking. But I probably also hurt her feelings a bit in the process.

"Stop looking at me like I'm a three-legged dog," I grumble.

"Sorry, I don't mean to be looking at you like...like that..." Gillian says, turning to look at the door as a customer walks inside and goes to meet Lola at the counter. "We're just...we want to help, Amy."

I don't say anything, rubbing some of the graphite on the page with my pinky finger so it smudges into threatening fog.

"This is your first big thing, you know? And we all want it to work out the way you want it to. It just sucks that sometimes we don't have control over how other people act or feel."

I stop for a second, dropping my pencil. "Do you think he's trying to let me down easy?"

Gillian hesitates. "I don't know that for a fact, but –"

"God, is that what he's doing?" I ask, voice quivering.

"I don't think so, but –'

'Because if that's what he's doing, I'll die. I'll just want to die," I say and then burst into loud, tremendous tears. I push my hands over my face and weep.

"Oh, honey, okay…" Gillian rubs my back. I hear her whisper over her shoulder to Lola and the customer, "Boy troubles."

Worse than boy troubles. Grown ass man with a child troubles. Grown ass man with a child and an ex-wife suing for *custody* troubles. I could go on and on. It only makes it sound worse.

"You let it all out…just cry it out."

I haven't really cried over it since it happened. A few tears shed while Hunter held my hands, telling me, "I'm not going away. This is just a bump in the road. I promise, I promise."

I don't believe in promises.

"Hunter is a good man. I know he is. And he cares for you. He will come back. He hasn't even really gone away…"

"We don't know that yet. He's barely even sent a text to me since he – he –" I can't get the words out through the sobs.

"He'll come back."

"People don't come back, Gillian," I snap suddenly, pulling away from her. "People never come back. You saw what happened with Mom."

Gillian blinks. "I…alright. That's different."

"It's not. That's our *mother,* and she walked away. Hunter's a guy I've been seeing for like a month!" It seems not only possible he'll walk away. It seems likely.

Gillian grabs my hand tight. "Listen to me, Amy."

I drag my eyes to meet hers.

"Hunter cares for you. I saw it in the way he looked at you the other night. I promise, it's not something he can just walk away from. If he has a heart, which he must since he has a little girl who is so happy and sweet, then he has a heart *for you.*"

It feels like I'm talking to the old Gillian. The one before Stella came along who was so passionate about love, who believed it existed. When Stella was born, she became all consumed with that. I guess I can understand Hunter's callous behavior when it comes to women, up until me. Gillian never even dated, never had the time.

Now that she and Axel have found their way to each other, the gleaming hope of true love and fairytales is back in her eyes.

I just don't know if I ever believed it. My sisters say our mom and dad were perfect together. Not to me. Never to me.

But why? What did I see that they didn't?

"The hardest thing is to just let go and trust that whatever is right will...will be."

I suck on my lower lip. Trust has never come easy to me. Not since Mom left.

"I know you're trying to figure out a way to argue with me, but..."

I laugh and lean my head on Gillian's shoulder, tears abated.

"You won't find a good argument for that."

"I want to know, Gilly."

She kisses the side of my head. "I know you do. It's okay. You'll get there."

I can only hope.

"Hunter couldn't have known she would show up, Amy. You're being cruel to yourself by telling yourself a story where Hunter is cruel. And I don't think he is. At least not what from what you've told me," Jordan posits.

I'm sitting in my normal spot, the one I've been in for years, talking through my non-breakup with Hunter. "I suppose."

"And you deciding to have sex with him...his pulling away isn't a punishment for that."

I let out a long sigh. "Thank you. I needed to hear that."

"Obviously, your feelings need to come first, but it might be worth imagining how hard it is for him to pump the brakes when it's clear he cares about you very much."

Jordan was thrilled to find out she was correct about the budding feelings between Hunter and me. She's been my therapy cheerleader. Always on my side to keep it real, but never afraid to say that she's excited for me.

When I came into her office today, I wasn't sure who was more upset over the news that things had gone semi-south between us, me or her. But, as usual, she's made me feel much better about the situation. Keeping me grounded.

"Amy," Jordan says with a soft smile. "It's not over. If it was over, he would have said he was ending things. And he told you he explicitly wasn't. The anxiety is natural, but you can't let it run your every thought."

"You're right."

We are silent for a minute. Sometimes in therapy, my mind drifts elsewhere completely. I'm thinking about going back home and heading up to my bedroom hurriedly so as to avoid any possible interaction with Hunter or Jessica that would surely break my heart.

Even in my room I'm not safe, though. From my bedroom window I can see his yard. I can see that goddamn gate.

The thought of it is like a shock to the heart.

"Where are you, Amy?"

My eyes flick to Jordan.

"You're thinking about something. What is it?"

I sigh. It feels stupid, but I have to say it. "I keep thinking about the gate."

"What about the gate?" Jordan asks.

Damn, I've mentioned it enough that she knows exactly what I'm talking about. "I don't know. It's strange, I just... when I see it, it makes me so mad. Even when things were safe and fine between us, it made me mad."

"It's like you've made it a symbol or something."

I nod. "Yeah. I guess so."

Jordan pauses. "You've lived in that house your whole life, Amy. Isn't it possible that you're reacting to something else?"

I shrug. "I don't know, I mean...the whole house ends up being a trigger sometimes. Making me think about my mom."

"That makes a lot of sense. You've made a lot of new memories there, but your earliest ones there were with her, after all."

I frown. "Sucks."

Jordan chuckles. "Yeah. It does suck. Spaces are... powerful. Now you've got a lot of Hunter attached to things. The neighborhood, the gate..."

I conjure an image of the gate in my mind. Stare hard at it. The first memory that comes to mind...it should be Hunter's former fling tripping into the yard or me sneaking through to make love to him just the other night.

There's an untouched memory coming through. Someone walking through the gate hurriedly from our yard into Hunter's.

Focus, Amy.

"I..." I close my eyes to concentrate harder. "I think..."

The person walking through the gate comes more into focus. A man. Trying to tuck in his shirt as he goes. Turning his head over his shoulder with a fleeting, nervous glance.

Oh my god. *Oh my god.*

My eyes pop open and my jaw drops. "Malcolm."

Jordan's forehead screws together, "Malcolm? You mean, your dad's friend who your mom had an affair with and then..."

"Yes! Yes, *that Malcolm.*" Malcolm, Grant, and Dad were all college friends. For years, Malcolm and my mother had an affair behind my father's back until it finally came to light. The second it did, Mom left with Malcolm and filed the divorce papers. They're married now.

A hideous couple.

"What about Malcolm?"

"I remember...seeing him go through the gate. When I was younger. I don't even think I knew what I was seeing." There was one summer all my sisters were in camps while I stayed home with Mom. I was learning to read and spent most of the time sitting at my desk going through picture books. Research now, I guess.

Malcolm would visit Mom quite a bit while Dad was at work. Didn't think anything of it then. In fact, I've blocked it out of my memory.

One afternoon, I remember seeing Malcolm hurriedly rushing through the gate in the back. I had no idea why, obviously. I was so little I didn't know the terrible things people can do to each other. Not a minute later, I heard the front door open and Dad's voice echo through the house, "Guess who's home early?!"

Maybe I forgot about it because deep down I knew. Maybe I forgot about it because right when Dad got home, I rushed down to greet him and then he took Mom and me out for ice cream, just the three of us (a rare treat as the youngest of five).

Maybe I forgot about it because Mom acted like nothing had happened.

She has always been a very good liar.

"Oh, Amy..."

I've been so lost in thought I've forgotten myself.

"You think it was..."

"It had to have been. Right?"

Jordan's eyes harden on me and then she nods. "It would make sense, regardless, that you would attach that memory to the trauma of your mom leaving."

I grip the couch cushion beneath me.

"No wonder seeing that woman walk through the gate brought up so much feeling in you."

My heart is pounding so hard. I'm both relieved that I finally understand and heartbroken to have found this memory.

"It's just a gate," Jordan says in her kindest voice. "It has ghosts attached, but the gate can't hurt you. The ghosts can't hurt you either."

I'd like to believe her. But I didn't even know I was haunted.

The time is up faster than I'd like it to be. Jordan offers for me to come back in an hour after her next session if I need to talk further, however, I think it's time to go bury myself in bed and never come out.

That feeling changes, though, when I check my phone after my therapy session and there's a text from Hunter.

I open it hurriedly.

> Hope you're doing well. Can I take you out
> Thursday night?

I press the phone to my chest. It's not over. Not yet.

One thing is for sure: I don't want to be haunted by any more ghosts. Hunter and Jessica will *not* become ghosts.

18

HUNTER

"You know, the custody portion wasn't too tricky with my divorce, but I wanted to be sure Aileen wasn't going to change her mind or do anything...stupid," Kent explains as he hands me a cup of coffee.

He sits beside me at his kitchen island. Feels a little wrong to be in Amy's house given the distance I'm trying to impart. But when I reached out to Kent about the situation with Veronica, he invited me over for coffee immediately.

"Amy's out for the day, so we can talk privately," he explained clearly.

Given how pressing the situation is on my heart, I was walking out the door before I hung up the phone.

Though Kent is only about a decade older than me, he feels like a father to me sometimes. He makes dad jokes, drinks drip coffee, needs people to explain to him what to do with his phone, and wears reading glasses that he looks over the rims of.

All these little things I never saw in my own father.

"He's the best of the best," Kent explains and then sips his coffee.

"I need the best of the best," I say. After going through my entire legal team, I realized I had no one involved in family law and my divorce lawyer retired and moved to Palm Springs.

Kent smiles softly. I can see the echo of Amy's smile in his. "I really don't think you have anything to worry about, Hunter."

"Don't courts always favor mothers?"

His eyes roll to the side. "Present mothers, sure."

I chew on my lower lip. "What if I'm not seen as a present father?"

"Oh, please. Why? Because you work? Someone has to work to take care of your daughter."

"Not every father runs a Fortune Five Hundred company..." Women are often indicted for working and having a family. Men not as often. However, single fathers come with a different level of scrutiny. I feel it constantly. With the Ricks group, I'm too soft. With the playgroups, I'm too disconnected. It's a rock and a hard place.

"Hunter, she's an addict."

I start to bring the cup of coffee to my lips, but the idea of drinking it makes my stomach turn. I haven't been able to eat since Veronica's unpleasant return. Now I can't drink coffee? This is worse than I thought. "I don't know. She seemed pretty clean."

"Once an addict, always an addict. Now, don't get me wrong, people can grow and change. It doesn't make them a bad person," Kent explains. "Of course not. But the addictive behavior will always be there. No one is going to grant her custody. Visitation, maybe, but –"

"I don't want that either." Perhaps that is harsh to most people. Why would I keep my daughter from her mother?

Well, I've seen a future with someone who has acted

more like a mother than Jessica's flesh and blood. Amy Solace would be mother enough. I know it.

I wouldn't want to force that on her. She's so young. I'm not in a rush.

But I can see it.

First, though, we have to get around this roadblock.

Kent nods. "Then you gotta give my guy a call."

I don't waste a second after Kent gives me the number. I dial the number of the lawyer, a guy by the name of Sam Serty. It's a direct line, bypassing any of that secretary junk, which is helpful.

"Serty."

I glance at Kent. Sam Serty sounds quite surly over the phone. "Hi, Mr. Serty. I was given your name by a former client of yours, Kent Solace, and –"

"Solace. Yes. Name rings a bell. And you are?"

"Sorry, where are my manners? This is Hunter Ricks."

Serty is quiet for a moment. "How can I help you, Mr. Ricks?"

"Well, I've got a bit of a custody dilemma for you."

Serty laughs heartily. "My favorite kind. Lay it on me."

I explain to him my situation. Veronica's absence, her addiction, her reappearance, my daughter, our bond, etcetera. I hear Serty tip tapping away on his keyboard taking notes as I speak, and from time to time, he hums as if I've said something groundbreaking. Kent eventually slips out of the kitchen to give me privacy.

"So, that's it," I say when my story finally comes to a close.

"You're not married, are you?"

I purse my lips. "No, I'm not...married."

"You dating?"

"I...date one woman in particular."

"Okay, that's good. That's a good start. Can you marry her soon?"

"No, I'm not going to – is my winning the case hinging entirely on if I'm married or not?"

Serty laughs. "No, no. It'd help, certainly, but no."

"You think she has a possibility of getting some sort of custody arrangement?" I ask, nervously twisting my mug on the counter.

"Well, listen, she still has her parental rights. And if she's clean, she can file for partial custody. Certainly couldn't get full, given her absence and her history, but I take it you don't want that."

"No. I don't. I don't even want her to get visitation if that's possible."

Serty clears his throat. "Okay, so we're going for a sort of scorched earth policy, huh? I like it."

"You'll take my case, then?"

"Absolutely. Any friend of Solace is a friend of mine, Mr. Ricks."

I try to resist a resigned chuckle. At the beginning of this call he barely recognized Kent's last name. Now they're "friends." Whatever. If he can get the job done, I don't need someone earnest.

"I'd like to meet you and your daughter as soon as possible. Tomorrow. Come into my office. We'll have lunch."

"That sounds great." I don't even bother to consider my schedule. This is top priority, above anything else.

"And that girlfriend of yours, she can come too."

I freeze. "Uhm – well –"

"Don't want to get her wrapped up in it? Alright. Fine. I get it. Tomorrow, Ricks. You're on my books."

I start to respond, but he hangs up before I can. I put the phone down and take a moment to breathe. I know I have everything under control as well as I can. But I can't help being frustrated there's anything to even get under control. Life was going perfectly. I was taking care of Jess, falling for Amy. That in and of itself felt like a lot to balance.

Now, all of that can slip away in the blink of an eye if I'm not careful.

I watch Amy push a meatball around her plate. She's barely eating. I'm barely eating. Our food has gone cold.

"How's the spaghetti?" I ask.

"Good," she replies with a small smile.

"Good."

The restaurant around us is just as quiet except for tinkling piano music playing over the loudspeakers. I thought it best to leave Jessica out of our dates for now. She's having a playdate with Stella at Axel and Gillian's house while Amy and I connect.

However, there is a significant lack of connecting right now.

It feels...awkward. Not in the sense that anything has changed, but it feels like there's a wall up between us that neither of us knows how to take down.

"How's your filet?"

I glance down at my filet mignon of which I've taken one bite. "Good."

"Good."

The only thing we've both managed to consume is our wine. We're splitting a bottle. About three quarters of it are gone.

Amy drains her latest glass and I immediately hold up the bottle. "More?"

"Please."

She holds out her glass and I tip the bottle in, watching the red wine slosh inside like a red sea.

"Did I...did I tell you how nice you look tonight?" I say softly.

Amy flushes. "About ten times already."

"Oh, well..."

She shrugs bashfully. "It's not like I get tired of hearing it."

"Well, it's about the only coherent thought I've managed to communicate aloud to you all night."

Amy lifts her eyes to mine, brown and wonderfully soft. I reach across the table, take her hand, and then kiss her knuckles. "You're beautiful, Amy."

She flushes.

"You're nervous, tonight."

She nods. "So are you."

I chuckle. "Is it obvious?"

"No, I just have to assume, given everything."

I purse my lips.

"We don't have to talk about it, I just –"

"No, it's the elephant in the room, that's for sure."

Our hands stay folded together on the tabletop. Amy watches my thumb travel across her skin. Back and forth, back and forth... "I wasn't sure if I'd hear from you again."

"Really?"

"I know, it's silly. You made it so clear that it wasn't a... breakup. But I couldn't help but worry that you might have gotten scared and had some –" Amy pauses. "Regrets."

I squeeze her hand. "No! No regrets. Of course not."

She sighs in relief. "Okay, good."

"I was thinking that *you* might have regrets given how... the other night on your birthday and –"

Amy shakes her head. "No, I don't have any regrets. Maybe if I hadn't heard from you, I would have, but..." She wraps her other hand around mine. "I'm glad we did that."

"Yeah?"

She grins. "Yes."

"You have no idea how much that means to me," I say. "Really, Amy. All I want is to make you happy." The second it comes out; it feels vaguely false. Not that I don't believe it. But I might not be able to. "It's just..."

Amy's face falls. "Complicated right now."

"Very."

A lock of her brown hair falls in front of her face as she looks down at her mostly uneaten spaghetti. "I know that Jessica comes first, Hunter. I have no illusions about your priorities. After all, we've only been seeing each other for a little over a month. That's no time at all." She raises her gaze and says with resignation, "I just don't want you to forget about me."

My head bobs back like the words have physically hit my forehead. "Forget about you? How could I possibly forget about *you*, Amy?"

"You're a busy man."

"So?"

Amy takes a deep breath. "I just mean, I'll wait. As long as I know there's a place for me in your heart, I'll wait."

"I adore you, Amy."

Her face lights up.

"You've got more than a place in my heart. You're rooted there."

"Oh...good."

I shake my head. "You're unbelievably cute, you know that?"

Her nose squinches up. "Hunter..."

"Sorry, can't help it. I see it, I say it."

Under the table, I feel her foot softly caress the inside of my calf. A strange, arousing closeness. Reminds me of my legs amidst hers. "I think I'm done with dinner," she says delicately.

"I'll pay the check and I'll take you home."

"You don't have to take me home. Not *right* home, at least."

I furrow my brow, unsure of her meaning, until she looks up at me and I see a match light in her brown irises. "Right...not *right* home."

"Not at all."

My eyebrows jump. "Who are you and what have you done with Amy Solace?"

Amy giggles. *There she is.* "I'm trying something new. Is it not working?"

"No, it's working, it's definitely..."

Amy's foot rises further up my leg.

I need to get that check.

I END up having to get up and track down the waiter. I hand him my card, give him an egregious tip for a meal we barely ate any of, and then hurry with Amy out to the valet.

We wait in silence, hand in hand, for the Hummer to pull up, and once it does, we scramble inside.

My heart is pounding. I can barely focus on the road when in my peripheral, Amy's silky blue dress is draped so perfectly over her thighs. "So, I'm not taking you home."

"No."

"Where should I take you?"

I see her widen her thighs in her seat. "Somewhere private."

This sort of excitement never goes away no matter how old I get. The anticipation of enjoying a woman. The trembling edge of flirtation. In fact, it's only gotten better with age.

Scratch that. It's gotten better *with Amy*.

"Hunter..." she says, her voice curling into a whine.

"What? What is it?"

"Just pull over."

I drive, wide-eyed. "You want me to pull over? Where?"

"Anywhere." In my peripheral, I see her hand slide down her thighs, caressing. That's where my hands should be. "I need you. I can't wait."

I'm a slave to desire. Not mine. Hers.

I turn down a darkened, residential side street and jerk the car over toward the curb. The second I put it in park, Amy throws herself on me, her lips finding mine in a passionate kiss. I don't even have time to take off my seatbelt before she does.

Her hands grab locks of my hair, pulling tightly. "God, I've missed you," she whispers.

"Amy –" I can't speak before her tongue slides into my mouth. *Oh my god*. This feels amazing.

In an awkward push and pull, we get her over the center console so she's sitting in my lap, straddling my thighs with her groin pressed to mine. "I can feel you," she murmurs.

My erection. "I'm sorry, it happened so fast, I –"

"No, I love it." She reaches for the spaghetti straps of her dress. "Feel me."

The bodice of her dress tumbles down, revealing her perky, bare breasts. "Holy, sh—" I'm cut off by my mouth connecting with her nipple. I roll my tongue around it while my hand massages her other breast.

Meanwhile, Amy begins to shift her hips back and forth against mine. My erection grows, pressing into the shallow haven of her panties. I moan, arousal climbing.

"Mm, that feels...g-good," Amy whimpers.

I pop my mouth off her breast. "I don't have a condom."

"Fuck, me either."

Dammit. "There are other things we can –"

"Don't men always have a condom. In their wallet?"

I laugh against her chest and speak between kisses to her clavicle and neck. "I didn't want to assume this would happen."

Amy presses her forehead to the crown of my head, gripping the base of my skull. "Hunter, I need you inside me. I need it so bad."

I slide my hands up her back, burying my face in the crook of her neck.

"I need to know that you care."

"I do. I've told you I do."

"But it's not the same. If it's not your body, it's just not the same."

I lift my chin to look into her eyes. Crammed here behind the steering wheel, the sex won't be as mind-blowing as I'd like it to be.

That's not the point, though, is it?

Amy needs reassurance. My body will do for her what my words can't.

"You can pull out," she says nervously.

"I haven't done that in years."

Amy laughs. "Does that mean you've forgotten how?"

"No," I reply with a smile.

We stare at each other, the silence somehow more oppressing in the hot car. I try to grab a kiss from her lips, but she jerks back. The seatbelt catches and pinches my chest. "Ow, fuck."

Amy unbuckles me, letting the strap slide into its holder with a whoosh. "There."

I run my hands up from her thighs to her ass over and over. "We have to be careful, honey."

"I know. I will be."

It's not her I'm worried about. It's me. Amy drives me fucking nuts. I might not be able to handle myself. But here she is, bare-chested and beautiful. On top of me. So close. So *ready*. And after everything the past few days, all the tension and the stress, I definitely need this just as much as she does.

So, I reach up, tangling my fingers through her hair, and pull her lips to mine.

As we kiss, I reach back to recline the seat back. Further and further until I'm laid out under her.

Amy undoes my belt buckle and tries to slide it off, but it's pinned underneath my weight. We both laugh and just leave it there, hanging open. "Sex in a car is not as easy in the movies."

"Oh, definitely not."

"But the windows actually fog up," she says with a giddy laugh. She reaches over and draws a quick heart on the window.

"God, how can you be so sexy and so cute at once?" I muse, working on undoing my pants.

"Probably has something to do with my tits being out."

"Come here, you."

It is a flurry of motion as we kiss and move our clothes

aside, trying to wriggle as best we can in the confines of the driver's seat. We juke and jive until our groins make naked contact. I immediately let out a moan. "Baby, you're wet."

"Obviously."

My heart pumps hard. The thought of being inside her *bare* is driving me crazy. "When I tell you to get off, you have to, alright?"

Amy nods and then raises her hips. I adjust my cock upward for her and with slinking elegance, she drops herself onto me.

It is a warm ecstasy, the feeling of her pussy clenching around me, my cock sliding directly against her wet walls.

"This...oh god, feels so g-good," she moans.

"You take control, baby. Take control."

It takes her a second to get her rhythm, unsure how to raise and lower her hips. I help her at first, guiding her up and down, up and down until she gets the motion engrained in her pelvis. Then, she's off to the races.

Amy places her hands on my chest and sits up straight. Her eyes are closed, intently focused on her thrusts.

"Yes, baby girl. That's it."

Her mouth falls open and she lets out a moan.

I stare at her tits as they bounce with each pulse. "Fuck, you're beautiful."

Amy smiles, eyes fluttering halfway open.

"You're beautiful and you feel – oooh –" A wave of euphoria beats up from my pelvis to my chest. My back lifts off the leather seat and I clench my teeth. "You feel so good."

"How are you doing?" Amy asks, touching my chin tenderly while she continues to fuck me.

"Holding on for dear life," I reply.

She laughs.

I need her to come before me. I can't do much for her after, given the circumstances. I grip her bottom, pressing her pussy flush to me. Amy gasps loudly, pressing her hand to the inside of the door.

I'm in control now. I pound my hips up into her, watching her jolt on top of me. A stumbling moan comes out of her mouth, her eyes wide. "What – what are you –"

I bet it feels different for her, being on top. I can get deeper, hit all those sensitive nerves in just the right way for her to –

"Ah – I'm – " Amy presses her chin to her chest and groans.

I feel the first clench of her pussy and that just about tips me over the edge. Have to hold on just one more second. "Off, Amy, *off.*"

She miraculously makes it off of my cock in the middle of her orgasm.

Without the pressure of her pussy and the friction of her thrusts, my impending release jerks just out of my reach. As if sensing my frustration, Amy presses her throbbing center against my cock, dragging it back and forth down the shaft.

Wordlessly, I thrust my hips with my cock squeezed between her lower lips. Once, twice, three times and then it happens.

I come on myself, onto the bottom of my shirt. My head snaps back as a punch of pleasure twists into my gut. Amy continues to press herself onto me, prolonging my release until there's nothing left and I've made a mess of myself.

Without my one track mind focused on coming, the world comes back into focus. All at once, I'm overheated. I turn the car back on and crank the AC. Amy laughs, her chest heaving up and down to catch her breath. "How do you feel?" she asks.

"Good!" I say with a first cup of coffee in the morning intonation. "Really...good."

"Sorry about your shirt."

I glance down at the slimy splotches on my shirt. "Oh, it's fine. More than fine." I'll have to do something about it before I get Jessica. But it's a small price to pay for being entwined with Amy Solace.

Amy leans down, lips searching for a kiss, which I give her without question.

"Did that show you? That I care?"

She smiles sweetly and nods. "Yes, thank you."

I almost say something I'd regret saying. Not because it's not true, but because it's impossible right now. What I want to say, though, is that I wish I could take her home with me. I wish I could take her home with me forever.

That night, however, is not tonight.

Soon. I pray that it's soon.

19

———

AMY

Though I don't see Hunter nearly as much as I did before Veronica's appearance, I see him enough to coast on the memories. I've made it a whole week at a time just remembering the feeling of his hand on my thigh or the way he says the word, "Beautiful," in his deep, yet delicate voice.

It's the first days of September. Labor Day weekend. Hunter decided to take Jessica away for a few days to visit the development of his newest venture down south. I didn't expect to be invited, nor was I. But I was certainly thrilled to hear Jessica ask if I could come when I said goodbye to them.

"Not this time, sweetie," Hunter said.

Not this time. That meant there'd be future times, didn't it?

They're coming back today and then Jessica starts her first day of pre-school tomorrow. A full day away from home, away from her daddy. I wanted to offer to help him with school pickup or keeping an eye on her in the afternoons but resisted. It didn't feel appropriate given his level of concern with the mounting custody case.

Still, though, I wish I could help that way. Resisting the closeness I feel to Jessica and Hunter is getting harder by the day, even if there are these new obstacles between us.

Anyway, with their return this afternoon, I've decided to leave a little surprise for Jessica on their front porch. I put together a basket full of different fun treats and activities from a new set of crayons (the biggest pack with all the colors she could hope for) to a few books for early readers to a Pez dispenser shaped like Cinderella, her favorite Disney princess. I've gussied it up with Easter grass and sparkly ribbon.

I walk through their front yard and up to the door, dropping it squarely on the welcome mat. I straighten out the ribbon, readjust a few of the treats, and then smile. I hope I have a lot more opportunities like this. To make things special for Jess.

"Oh. It's you."

A chill runs down my spine. I turn around to see Veronica standing at the foot of the stairs leading up to the porch. "Hello there!" I say, standing up and straightening out the wrinkles in my dress. "Veronica, right?"

She smiles. "We don't have to pretend like we don't know each other."

I swallow. "Right..."

"Cute basket."

"Thanks. It's Jessica's first day of school tomorrow, so I thought I'd drop off a little – I guess, a care package. You know?"

Veronica's eyes tighten at the corners. "Sweet of you."

"Oh, it's nothing."

She stands there, unmoving.

"What about you? What are you doing here?"

"Well, I wanted to drop by to see my daughter, of course. But every time I've been by this past week –"

"They're on a trip."

Veronica raises her head sharply. "Of course. His little flavor of the day knows that and I don't."

Flavor of the day. I know she's saying that to get under my skin. But it still stings, especially remembering his string of ex-lovers.

"Anyway, if Jessica has school tomorrow, I'm sure they'll be back today." Veronica traipses over to the wicker bench on the porch. "I'll wait here. I brought a book." She whips out a brightly-covered novel, one that's been on the front tables of every bookstore I've had a reading at.

Dammit. I inadvertently gave away when Hunter would be back. Although, as is the case with bed bugs, Veronica would manage to catch him at some point. Was only a matter of time. I can't just let her sit here, though. I have to do something. At least attempt to. *Don't be a coward, Amy. She's just a woman.* I don't know much about her. Other than her role in Hunter and Jessica's life. Who knows? Maybe she's dangerous. Or maybe she just needs one more person to let her know what her place is around here. "I can't imagine Hunter would appreciate you waiting around for him."

Veronica lifts her eyes from her book. "You're speaking on behalf of him now?"

I screw my lips together.

"Goodness gracious, you've got it bad for him, don't you? What is he, twice your age?"

"Not *twice*." Not quite nearly. But...older still by a mile.

"Oh, sweetie, you've barely been around the block. You have no idea what a man like Hunter is capable of."

I scoff. "Your attempts to intimidate me are –"

"Not attempts to intimidate. Not at all. Woman to woman, I'm warning you..." Veronica's tone of voice has shifted to something, dare I say, almost motherly. Her smile is wan as she speaks. "Men like Hunter, they pick who they want and they use them up until they've gotten their fill. Take it from me. I would know."

I narrow my eyes. "*You* left *him*."

"Yes, I did. Because I wasn't ready to be what he needed me to be. So, I left. I was the bigger person."

"I'd hardly call 'abandoning' your child being the bigger person."

"He got her, didn't he?" Veronica asks.

I pause.

"Got to watch her grow up. Be the father he wanted to be for her. Didn't have me in the way." Veronica looks off into the distance and sighs, an abused heroine in a soap opera. "I'm just letting you know. Would hate for another star to dim."

I resist rolling my eyes. "I'm going to warn him you're here."

"That's just fine. Where else could he possibly go?" she asks, leaning back in the settee and tucking herself back into her book. "Good to see you again..." She trails off. She doesn't even know my fucking name.

"Amy."

Her eyes flick to me briefly. They scald every inch of my skin. "It's cute you think I care to remember."

I open my mouth to respond but my jaw tenses before I can speak. She doesn't deserve another moment of my time. Not another word. As quick as I can, I dart back to my house, my pulse not settling until I'm in past the front door with all the locks set.

Something about that woman is terrifying. Insidious. I

swear, it's not just because she's threatening Hunter and Jessica, my future. I bet if I walked past her on the street, she'd still terrify me.

"Dropped off the basket?" I hear Dad call out from the kitchen.

I force a smile. "Yep. All ready."

The hairs on the back of my neck will not go down no matter how I try to distract myself. Drawing doesn't help. Neither does talking with Kira while she takes her lunch break. I can't even drown out my feelings and take a nap. I just toss and turn.

What does Veronica mean that he'll use me up? She can't possibly believe that's what happened to her, can she?

Unless there's something Hunter is hiding. A darkness veiled beneath his charm.

Is it possible he just wants me for now? Until the next younger, prettier thing turns his head?

But Jessica...she knows about me. She cares for me.

I'm not just a name on his roster, hidden from daylight.

No matter how logically I spell this out, I can't manage to settle my nerves. I just need to see him. I need to know more.

I need to know who the hell Veronica really is.

20

HUNTER

"God, this tie is itchy," Drew complains, pulling at the red wool necktie I loaned him so he could gain admittance to the club.

I laugh. "Not used to a dress code, huh?"

He flushes and glances at Axel and Grant. "My circles tend to be a little less formal."

Our attire isn't terribly formal, but the club demands a coat and tie. Loafers are also a must, but Drew got in with a pair of fashionable sneakers.

"The club" is the Ash Club, a members-only men's club of the days of old. It's an invite-only sort of place; my membership has been grandfathered in by, well, my grandfather. The Ricks men have been members since the founding of the club.

Today is an "invitation day" when we're allowed to bring prospective candidates of the club to enjoy all its amenities and entreaties in the lush Grande Lounge, as it has been aptly titled. Cherry leather couches and armchairs, paintings of hunting scenes and the founding members on the wall, chandeliers dripping with yellowing light from the rafters.

Our visit is being accompanied by a concert pianist who has a performance later this evening at the Philharmonic. Those musicians. Anything for a buck.

I needed a day with the guys. Gillian asked Axel if I could include Drew in the fold even though he's still on the periphery of being Dana's object of affection. Still, he's easy enough to get along with, I thought the more, the merrier.

Plus, that way I can get the most intel possible on the Solace girls.

"Anyway, Nobu is out. Gillian isn't interested," Axel mumbles, grabbing his glass of scotch off an antique end table I'm certain would cost at least a hundred k at auction.

"You couldn't have possibly thought she would be. That's not Gillian's style at all," Grant scolds.

"No, I know, but it's Nobu! How could she not like Nobu?"

"Maybe because she isn't a Kardashian?" I reply dryly.

Axel rolls his eyes. "The Kardashians aren't the only people who dine at Nobu. Anyway, I'm out of ideas."

"This is SoCal. How are you out of ideas?" Drew says.

"Listen! I've been under a lot of pressure. I went from a bachelor to an engaged dad in two seconds! Give me a break."

Drew, Grant, and I exchange looks. Best to give the guy a second to breathe. "What about the roof at Ricks Melrose?" I offer and pull out my phone to navigate to the bookings for Ricks Melrose. "What's the date again?"

"Hunter, please, that's not necessary."

Grant hits Axel's knee. "Don't be silly. It's perfect. Gillian would love that. What with all the foliage and –"

"And there's the water feature," Drew exclaims.

I smirk his way. Even an engineer has seen pictures of the lavish Ricks rooftop on Melrose. "Plus," I add with a waggle of my eyebrows, "that way, I don't have to figure out what kind of gift to get you guys. Now. The date."

Axel blushes. "The twenty-first."

I tap off a message to my assistant to get the event booked and put my phone away. "There. Done."

Axel covers his face with his hand. "Oh god. She'll kill me for deciding without her."

"No, she won't," Drew replies, looking up from his phone. "I already texted her. She says it's a great idea."

"You have a texting relationship with Gillian?" Grant asks.

"Don't say it like that, man," Axel mutters. "You make it sound...romantic."

Drew looks back at his phone and shrugs. "I text all the Solace girls. I mean, not regularly, but –"

"You're rubbing elbows with all her sisters and yet you're still terrified to put the moves on Dana, huh?" Grant asks, resting his elbows on his knees, studying Drew like he's a bug in a museum.

Drew frowns. "I can be friends with my friend's siblings."

"Sure you can," I say with a nod.

"Why did you say it like that, though?" Drew retorts.

"I just said 'sure you can'," I repeat.

"But you're saying it like you're not saying something else. And I know what you're all thinking, but nothing is happ –"

"How long have you been saying 'nothing is happening'?! Years now!" Axel exclaims.

Drew sinks into his chair, crossing his ankle at the knee

which reveals his mismatched socks. "I don't want to talk about it."

"I'll go, then," I say with a sigh. We've been doing a round robin of our problems. Grant started by discussing Tana's recent sleep regression, followed by Axel with the planning of the engagement party. Moving clockwise in the circle, Drew would be the next candidate. Now, though, with his embargo on discussing the Dana situation, it's my turn. "I'm fucking terrified," I say through a casual laugh.

"Cigars, gentlemen?" a server approaches with a silver tray of the finest smelling cigars.

Drew shoots up and takes one. "You can smoke in here?"

"It's a gentleman's club. Of course you can," Axel says.

We all take a cigar, let the server clip them, and then pass around a lighter. I don't smoke on the regular, but a nice cigar is an indulgence I find myself enjoying very occasionally.

I puff out the smoke and clear my throat. "Anyway..."

"You'd be an idiot not to believe you're going to win this case, man," Grant says, picking up where I left off.

"I don't know. Courts favor mothers," I reply.

"They don't favor addicts, though," Grant retorts.

I sigh. "Fair...I just...God, everything was going so well. Jess was doing good and things with Amy –"

"Can still go well," Drew intercedes.

I harden my gaze on the ember of my cigar. "I feel like I'm hurting her."

Out of the corner of my eye, I see the guys exchange glances.

"What's that look?" I ask.

"Nothing," Axel replies firmly.

"*Axel*...don't you think we should –"

I raise my eyebrows in alarm. "What's going on?"

"Everything is *fine*," Axel says through grit teeth, glaring at Drew.

Drew looks to Grant for backup, but Grant remains mute. Then, he looks at me. "Amy isn't sleeping."

"What?!" I cry out while simultaneously, Axel mutters, "Dammit, Drew. I promised Gill I wouldn't say anything!"

"He should know," Drew says. "She's not sleeping. She's stressed."

I look to Grant for more information. He can't be impartial Switzerland for too long. He sighs, pushing back a swath of hair from his forehead. "Kira's been sleeping with her most nights. Sometimes, Dana."

I can barely believe my ears. It's not that the news comes as much of a shock. I knew all of this was weighing on her quite nearly as heavily as it weighs on me. But to not be sleeping? Why didn't she tell me?

What's even more mortifying is all my friends know. And I didn't. Her own boyfriend.

If that's what I still am to her. Or what I've ever been…

"You all knew."

"Well, Amy didn't tell us. That's not how we knew," Drew says as if reading my mind of the deep patheticness I feel.

I run my hand through my beard. It's gotten too long. A little unkempt. Stress will do that. "I'm letting Veronica get in the way."

"She understands, man," Drew continues, trying to cheer me up.

"But she's suffering. Because of me. Because she cares about me. That's…"

"Don't you dare do something stupid like push her away," Axel says, waving his cigar through the air. "I did that and look at what that got me. I missed out on a lot of good years because I got scared."

I can make excuses for Axel's terror. He was still in his twenties. Me, I'm an old man by those standards. In my forties. Not only would it be immature to push Amy away, it would be a poor representation of what I can handle.

Before anyone can say another word, I get distracted by a familiar figure passing by. I incline my head back and smile at the dark-haired man. "Orlie Wynters?"

Orlie stops and turns to look at me. The man hardly smiles, but I manage to perk his lips up. "Ricks. What a surprise!"

I stand and give him a hearty shake. "Can't be that much of a surprise, can it?" I say, glancing at the portrait of the clubs' founders in which both our grandfathers are represented."

He rolls his eyes. "Well, I don't take chance meetings for granted."

"Let me introduce you. These are my friends Axel Hitchens, Grant Neville, and Drew Young."

Orlie nods at them. If he recognizes any of their names, he doesn't portray it on his face. "Pleasure."

The guys all say their hellos before I sweep back in. "Orlie just took over for his father at Wynters Corp."

"Well, it's just the beginning of a transition. Will be several years before I actually stand at the helm," Orlie says.

Grant and Axel exchange a look. "Wynters, huh?" Axel asks carefully.

"Yes."

"You know Kira, then," Grant adds.

"Kira..." Orlie narrows his eyes. "Kira Solace?"

Grant nods.

"Of course I know Kira. She's created our top performing applications."

Only Orlie Wynters would say "applications" instead of apps.

"We're…" Axel points between himself and Grant, "her brothers-in-law." Then he glances at Drew and me. "Guess we all are."

Drew kicks Axel's ankle.

Orlie's eyebrows jump. "Didn't know you were married, Ricks."

"No, no. Axel is just jumping the gun, aren't you, Ax?" I say with a glare.

Lucky for me, Orlie isn't the type to pry. We have a mutual respect as heirs to business dynasties. Neither of us likes people meddling in our business unless invited. For now, that's not a door we're going to open for each other.

We chat for a bit longer before Orlie excuses himself due to the smoke collecting. "Not good for my lungs," he says.

"Ours either," I reply.

He half-smiles and then hurriedly waves. "Next time, Ricks."

Once he's out of earshot and I'm settled back into my chair, Grant smiles slyly. "Wait until Kira gets word that Orlie's talking her up."

I raise an eyebrow.

"She *hates* him," Grant adds, mouthing the word hates so it doesn't somehow carry all the way across the room and down the hall.

"Ah…"

Conversation continues easily, as it always does with us guys. We hop from topic to topic, some of it meaningful, most of it not. I try to stay present, but it feels like frosted glass has gone up between me and the rest of the world. I'm desperately trying to look in and can't. Everything's obscured by my current circumstances.

And Amy...all that stress. Over me.

My poor girl. She doesn't deserve that. I know I'll hurt her if I leave...but it seems like I'm hurting her by staying too.

What the hell am I supposed to do?

21

———

AMY

"There you go! You're doing it!" I exclaim, stepping back from the swing set.

Jessica is pumping her legs hard and flying back and forth, higher and higher. She laughs loudly, her dark hair flying out of her face. "Daddy, look! I'm doing it!"

Hunter stands on the opposite side of the swing set, ducking out of the way as Jessica flies toward him. We were pushing Jess back and forth between us until I got the idea it was time for her to learn how to swing on her own. It took a couple tries, but now she's got it down to a science. There's power in those little legs. "I see that! Wow!"

Then, he smiles over at me. I smile back even though I feel rather nauseous about everything. Nauseous in the way you feel when you've overeaten. Full to the brim with confusion and desperation for things to be settled again.

We've been at the park for an hour now. Hunter invited me on the spur of the moment, waving at me over the fence to ask if I wanted to come. "Per Jessica's request."

But what about *his* request? He must have wanted me to come to invite me. He could have told her no. Right?

Hunter has been getting harder and harder to read as the days pass. I thought, with time, we would be able to let the Veronica thing drift into the background of our relationship. Instead, it seems to be moving forward each and every day. He's distracted. Quiet.

A bit like how things used to be.

I can't say I'm helping matters, though. Ever since I ran into Veronica a week ago, I've been on edge. I know I shouldn't believe a person with a character like Veronica's. She's not trustworthy. And yet, the things she said spoke to the Hunter I knew before we fell into our aching, desperate relationship. That Hunter who had a list of women he could rotate through so he didn't have to see someone twice in one week.

What about me? When will I get added to the list?

"I'm flying!" Jessica squeals.

Thank god for Jessica. She's the one keeping me firmly tethered here. The one part of this I don't have to question. "Yes, you are! It's a bird, it's a plane...no! It's Jessica!" I cry out.

She laughs again. Her laugh is a balm to my heart.

Hunter rounds the swing set and stands next to me, crossing his arms over his chest. Maybe he doesn't know what to do with his hands either. I slip mine into the pockets of my dress. "Thanks for coming," he murmurs softly.

I glance at him with a smile. "You're welcome."

His warm caramel eyes catch mine; my heart races, but I don't deign to look away. "She's been asking for you."

"Well, you know I'm just next door."

Hunter breaks eye contact first, looking at the toe of his shoe as he drags it through the mulch. "You've been a little harder to catch."

I hadn't noticed that. But yeah. I guess I have been. I'm slower to respond to texts and I've been out with Fiona more, brainstorming ideas for my book. My publisher is getting huffy with me after the past couple months of churning out idea after idea they deem too dark. I'm losing my touch.

"You're not avoiding me, are you?"

I could ask him the same question. "Just giving it all some space."

Hunter chews on his lower lip. "We never talked about the Veronica thing."

Which thing? I'm tempted to ask. However, I know exactly what he's referring to. I had sent him the warning text, as promised. In response, all I got was a thumbs up reaction to the message. "What is there to say?"

"Well, are you okay? I can't imagine she was too friendly...not really her M.O."

I glance at Jessica, still obliviously flying through the air. "Don't worry about me. In regard to Veronica at least."

"Amy, I am worrying about you," he says, brow hardening.

I sigh.

"Did she say something about me?"

My face betrays my desire to hide my thoughts, eyebrows rising, jaw dropping slightly ajar.

Hunter's shoulders tighten. "You know she'll say anything to make me look bad."

"Of course. That's why it wasn't worth bringing up," I reply.

"Are you watching?!" Jessica cries out.

"Yes, we're watching, sweetheart!" I say in response and, when she flies back, catch her at the top of her swing and give her a big push. She lets out a burbling laugh. A much needed moment of levity.

"What'd she say?" Hunter asks urgently.

I shake my head. "It was noth –"

"*Bullshit*," Hunter spits.

I recoil from him slightly, quickly making sure Jessica didn't overhear him.

Hunter takes a few deep breaths, closing his eyes tightly. "Sorry. I'm sorry."

"It's okay."

He gulps, protruding Adam's apple rolling up the front of his neck. "Please, just tell me what she said. It would make me feel so much better. And maybe I could make *you* feel better about it too."

In my mind, if I say it out loud, that means it's a threat. Keeping it in, it's just a delusion. I nod toward a bench facing the swing set. "Let's sit."

We bid Jessica to keep going as long as she likes (hopefully, a while on those little legs) and cross to the bench where we plop down and fall into silence.

Hunter watches me. Waiting.

"She just said some nasty things about how you're going to use me up and discard me. Like you did her."

Hunter balks. "I didn't do that to –"

"I know, I said as much to her. Don't worry, I was defending you."

He grimaces, staring across the playground. "You shouldn't have had to do that."

"Of course I do. You're my..." What *is* he to me? "We're dating. I know that's not what you did."

Hunter smiles sadly and reaches for my hand. For some reason, I have the impulse to draw it away from him.

Fuck. She's gotten in my head.

I don't, of course, letting him take my hand into his broad palms, caressing it gently. "I know you don't have a lot to go off. My track record is...spotty, at best. But you know how I feel about you, right?" Hunter kisses my hand tenderly.

I force a smile. "Of course."

"Amy."

"Hm?"

"Look at me."

I let my eyes meet his. It takes every bit of strength in me to look at him and not see a wolf that might swallow me whole. *Shit.* This is exactly what I didn't want to happen.

"You're still not saying something," he says solemnly.

"That's all that happened, I promise."

"No, not that. I believe that. It's..." Hunter sits up straighter, inclining his head to the side as he examines my expression. "You don't believe me."

I tear my eyes away. "No, that's not it."

"Then why have you been avoiding me?"

"You did it first."

"But I told you why. I explained. You know how hard I'm trying to be here for you."

I close my eyes and take a deep breath. "I know. I know how hard you're trying. She just got in my head. That's all. I need some time to recuperate. That's all."

Hunter does not take this well. He frowns. "You believe her over me."

"That's *not* what I said."

"Then how could she have gotten in your head?"

I have to maintain an even keel. We're in public for one. And Jessica is right across from us. While she might be in her own little world, all it would take is one look at us to see we're fighting. She doesn't deserve that. "I'm younger than you. Less experienced. Surely, it's fair for me to worry that your intentions are –"

"Haven't I shown you that you don't have to worry? With my actions?"

"I'm just a human, Hunter. I can know things with my brain and not feel them in my heart."

His grip loosens on my hand. "I see."

Dammit. That's not what I meant. I touch my chest meaningfully. "I feel things for you. Very deeply. It all moved so fast. I'm scared. That's all."

Hunter rips his eyes from mine. A punishment. "I understand."

I wait for him to look at me again. He doesn't. I lean over and kiss his cheek softly, the bristles of his beard rubbing my lips. I tighten that loosened grip of our hands. "Hunter...be patient with me. Please."

I thought I'd be begging for him to be patient as I got my body ready to have sex for the first time. But that happened much faster than anticipated. Now, I'm begging him to wait for me to trust him fully again.

"I know you haven't been sleeping, Amy," he says softly, gripping the revelation from thin air.

I withdraw, wide-eyed. Who told him? A classic grapevine of Solace sisters?

Hunter eyes roll over to mine. "I can't have you losing sleep over me."

"How do I stop this thing?!" Jessica yelps as she rides the air back and forth.

I leap up and rush over, a smile plastered on my face for her. "Stop pumping your legs first!"

In one smile for Jessica, I can push down every fear I have about what Hunter's just said. At least until later, in bed, when inevitably I will toss and turn for an hour before sneaking into Kira's room so that someone can comfort me back to sleep.

22

HUNTER

"That's a lot of books," Veronica remarks, looking at Jessica's bookcase across from her bed.

"I love books," Jessica says better than a docent in a museum. "They're in alphabetical order. By last name."

"I bet your daddy helped you with that, huh?" Veronica replies.

I have to give it to Veronica; she could be a helluva lot worse with her daughter than she is. That being said, I can tell Jessica is playing coy. She's not as shy as she usually is, just withheld. I didn't even have to coach her to do that. She can just tell that things are off.

"Yes, he calls it my library."

Veronica eyes the hand painted sign I ordered from someone off Etsy that indeed says, "Jessica's Library" in light pink cursive. "Yes, I see that."

This visit wasn't my idea. Obviously. However, given the original custody agreement that came about in our divorce, Veronica is legally allowed visitation. She of course never took advantage of that until now, and my lawyers and

I were foolish enough not to seek out a no-contact order. So, with her lawyers and the court involved, Veronica has been granted limited visitation with Jessica leading up to the trial. All my lawyers could do to fight it was stipulate that I must be there to supervise.

No issue with that, of course.

"Would you like a tour?" Jessica asks, gesturing to the shelf.

"Of your…of your bookshelf?" Veronica asks.

Jessica nods.

"Um. Sure."

I resist snorting. She has no idea what kind of patience you have to have with children and their hyper fixations. I predict Jessica will be talking about her books for the better part of the hour, leaving Veronica in a tumult of yawns.

That's my girl.

As she starts at the top at Aesop, I'm distracted by my phone buzzing in my pocket. I pull it out, set to immediately hang up on the caller. However, the name makes me take pause. Hank Turpin.

As per the advice of my custody lawyer, Sam Serty, I've hired a private investigator to look into Veronica's background. Where she's been the past few years, where she is now, who the hell this guy is that she's supposedly getting married to. So far, he hasn't come up with much, other than a stint in rehab about a year after Jess was born.

This could be important. In fact, if it's juicy enough, I probably have grounds to ask Veronica to leave my house right this second.

"Take it."

I look up to find Veronica staring at me.

"I know the business always comes first. We'll be fine.

She's just showing me her books, Hunter," she says with a smirk.

I glance at Jessica who is fiddling with her step stool in order to reach the top shelf. "Just one minute."

"As many as you like."

I narrow my eyes at her. "Leave the door open."

"Of course," Veronica says innocently.

"And don't..." It's no use giving her instructions. She's just going to be a contrarian or play the lost lamb card. "Jess, I'm going to be in the hall taking a phone call, okay?"

"Kay," she replies, tucking her tongue out of her mouth as she reaches for a book on the top shelf.

Veronica rushes in to her aid. "Here, honey, let me help you with that."

At least she's good for something.

I step out into the hall, far enough that I can't be over-heard, but close enough that I'll overhear if anything happens between Jessica and Veronica.

"Ricks," I say as I answer the phone, trying to put on my best "business" voice. After all, Veronica assumed I was taking a business call.

"Hiya, Ricks, how are you doing? It's Hank Turpin."

"Well. How are you?"

Hank sighs. I hear his chair creak in the background. I've never met the man, but from the picture Sam showed me on his website, he's a heavyset guy that could compete with the best of the old gumshoes. "Been better, been better."

"You have updates on our...project?" I say, glancing over my shoulder at the doorway.

"Not much for you, I'm afraid. Followed that lead out to Santa Barbara but it was a dead end. Still working on getting in contact with that old roommate she had after rehab, but –"

"We're in the red, you're saying."

Hank snorts. "You're all business, aren't you, Mr. Ricks?"

If only he knew how subtle I'm trying to be, he'd understand my use of businesslike epithets. "Just give it to me straight."

"Well," the investigator sighs. "I'm not giving up. I'm still trying to track down information on her fiancé. I called Stanford and they have no record of a Greer Daniels. So, that's a good start. Of course, he could be using a fake name if he's that type, but..."

Greer Daniels. Just another version of Hunter Ricks, in a way. I've seen a couple pictures of the guy. Suave and overly tan with veneers. Supposedly comes from money.

But people who have made their money illegally always say they're old money. New money would be too suspicious.

"How optimistic should I be?" I ask, hearing a peel of forced laughter from the other room.

"Oh. Very. Very optimistic."

From his tone, I am not very optimistic.

"Your case is top of mind for me. My number one priority."

It better be for how I'm paying him.

"I just wanted to be in touch. Call any time. Especially if you get any new leads."

"Will do. Thank you for your –"

I'm interrupted by a terrifying screech of, "*What?!*" from the other room. Veronica's voice when she's angry is horrendously shrill.

I don't bother with the pleasantries of a goodbye to

Hank, hanging up and hurrying back into the room. "What's going on?!" I exclaim. My eyes immediately find Jessica. She's pressed up against the wall in fear, holding one of her books to her chest, staring at Veronica in fear.

Veronica snaps around to face me, anger blazing in her eyes. "What have you been telling her?"

I ignore her question, pushing past her to get to Jess. The second Jessica is in my arms, she starts to cry. "You can't yell at her, Veronica."

"I most certainly can when she says things that are abject *lies*."

"It's not a lie!" Jessica sobs.

"Not if that's what your daddy has been telling you," Veronica replies bitterly.

"*Veronica*. Enough."

She freezes at my admonishment.

"What happened?"

Veronica steps toward the bookshelf and pulls one of the books off. "I asked Jessica to show me her favorite book. She said these were her favorite. Can you guess why?" She shoves the book toward my face.

It's one of Amy's books. Surely merely seeing her name didn't send Veronica into a tailspin, did it?

"Why don't you tell your father why you like them so much, Jessica?" Veronica taunts.

I put my hand out to distance her from me. "Do not speak to her like tha –'"

"Because..." Jessica says something, but it's garbled in my neck.

"What, sweetie?" I ask tenderly. "I couldn't hear you."

Jessica, my tiny little girl who has been shy her whole life, suddenly lifts her head and looks at Veronica. "Because my mommy wrote them."

My blood runs cold.

Veronica lifts her head proudly. "Now you can understand why I reacted the way I did, can't you?"

The expression on her face transports me back in time. That distant assuredness. Unafraid to hurt feelings.

It's the same face she wore when she abandoned Jessica.

She hadn't even lost all the postpartum weight yet, her stomach still a slight bubble under her loose dress. It had only been a month. A month of being parents.

Veronica had done her dark hair in loose curls. Her makeup was pristine.

And I could smell Jessica's diaper needed to be changed as she practically dropped my one-month-old into my arms the second I walked in from the office.

"I'm done, I think," she said coldly.

I didn't quite understand.

So, she spelled it out for me.

"I don't want to be a mother anymore."

I didn't react fast enough. That was always my biggest regret. That it took me too long to process, and by the time I was groveling after her, she was halfway down the driveway. How was I going to care for our daughter alone? I was still just a shell of myself, a few months after the tragic passing of my parents. I had the company to deal with. And a child. I needed help somewhere.

She said she didn't care.

I thought it might be post-partum depression. In fact, I'd been suspecting it. I offered to get her help.

If it was PPD, Veronica didn't want to try and fix it. She just wanted to leave.

And as she left me in the driveway of the old house, clutching our baby with the spoiled diaper, something always struck me.

Jessica didn't cry.

It's like she knew we were better off. Even when she was barely out of the womb.

Here I am again. Veronica proud for her cruelty. My daughter in my arms. This time, she can understand that she has nothing to lose in casting Veronica aside.

"I'm your mother, Jessica," Veronica says.

Jessica shakes her head.

"I am. Whether you like it or not. I carried you."

"I don't care. Amy is my mommy. Right, Daddy?" Jessica looks at me and touches my cheek. "Amy's my mommy."

I can't confirm or deny. "Veronica, I think you should go."

Her jaw tightens. "You're feeding her lies."

"I'm not –"

"And you can be sure I'll be using this in court."

I remain silent. I'd expect nothing less.

"Don't bother walking me out. I know the way." Veronica starts out of Jessica's bedroom and then stops. She turns, forcing a saccharine smile. "I'm sorry, sweetheart. Mommy's feelings are just hurt."

Jessica pulls her face into my neck, unable to watch the horror movie unfolding in front of her.

"I hope you can understand. We'll try again another time."

Fat fucking chance.

I don't feel safe until I hear the front door slam after Veronica. I cradle Jessica in my arms, and though she's grown, she feels as small as she was three years ago.

"Amy *is* my mommy, Daddy," she whimpers adamantly.

"Shhh, sweet pea..."

"*She is.*"

I'd love to tell her that she's correct. Nothing would make me happier than building that kind of life with Amy.

But *I* barely know where I stand with Amy, let alone my daughter.

One thing at a time.

23
___

AMY

ANOTHER DAY, ANOTHER REJECTION.

"We're not doing a story about Petunia's dad getting a girlfriend," Kris says sternly. She isn't doing her usual placating routine, throwing a Kitty in here and there. "Especially if the dad and girlfriend aren't together in the end."

I gulp and eye Fiona across the table. "It's real, though."

"We write children's books, Amy," Kris replies, her consonants aspirating tightly in her posh British way. "Christ, you'd think this is *Chicken Soup for the Soul,* the stories you're spouting off."

I take a deep breath. "Children deal with real problems."

"Yes, you're right. And at the end of the day they like to crawl in bed and read about their friend Petunia and all her fun hijinks so they can rest and relax knowing that life isn't all that hard, eh?" Kris snaps back.

I've never heard Kris angry. Doesn't usually come with the territory of publishing children's books.

"Tell her, Fiona."

Fiona looks at me sheepishly. She's the one I've been

batting ideas around with. She thought this one might work. "It is a little...dower."

Traitor.

"Understatement of the century," Kris snorts.

"Well, I'm sorry, but I can't be creative if I'm not writing what's truly inside me," I reply, trying my best not to let my racing emotions come forward.

"You don't need to be creative. You have to write the damn book, Kitty."

There's that Kitty we know and love.

"So, what you're saying is..." I've got to be careful about this. Last thing I want to do is have Kris throw me to the wolves. "I need to ignore my inspiration and write something that will sell you books."

"Precisely!"

Ah, capitalism. A joy.

"You've got it, Kitty. Now." Kris gets to her feet, grabbing her personalized leather portfolio off the table. "I've got another meeting to get to, but I'm sure Fiona will be happy to sit and have you bounce ideas off of her so that you can find the exactly right next upbeat happy not at all traumatizing idea for Petunia's next adventure!" She throws the door open and waves over her shoulder. "Ciao!"

Fiona and I are silent for a good minute as I clean up the sample drawings I brought for the book I just pitched. *Petunia's Paternal Partner.* The name isn't catchy, I know. Gotta work on it. But it's all a work in progress.

Including me.

"I'm sorry, Amy, I thought –"

"It's fine. I don't want to talk about it," I say coldly.

Fiona sighs. "You don't want to go through some ideas?"

"No, I don't. I am out of ideas. I'm out of –" I let out a

frustrated grunt. "I have nothing left to give. Not to you, not to anyone."

Fiona's eyebrows raise. "Oh."

I slump my shoulders. Every day, I've been shrinking. Further and further until there will be nothing left of me to give anyone. "I have to go."

"Okay, well, I'll call you later if –"

"I won't want to talk about Petunia later. Maybe Petunia's done," I say flippantly.

"You can't mean that, Amy."

I shrug, gathering up my purse and portfolio. "I don't know."

Fiona is reduced to silence, finally. I mutter a soft goodbye as I leave, clutching the folder of sketches to my heart.

When will I get to tell *my* story?

MOUNTAIN AIR DOES something for the lungs. Reaches down and tickles the insides, reminding us what it's like to breathe.

When Dad asked me if I wanted to go for a hike, I nearly said no.

I'm glad I didn't.

I've been leading the way up to Verdugo Peak. First time I'm the leader on this one. Behind me, I hear Dad panting.

"Damn, Ames, you're moving so fast."

I laugh and stop, putting my hands on my hips. "You want to stop for some water?"

Dad nods eagerly. When he reaches me, he drops his

backpack to the ground and pulls his tall water bottle out of the side pocket.

"I can carry that if you want."

"No, I'm fine, I'm..." He huffs as he sits on a rock. "I'm fine."

I smile and take a seat next to him. I could keep going. But I've got to keep pace with Dad. He's getting older. And I know he's starting to get self-conscious of it, especially now that he's a grandfather twice over. No need to make things worse.

"Thanks for coming with me, kiddo. I needed you here," he says.

"Ah, you would have been fine on your own."

"Maybe, but..." Dad eyes me nervously and then opens his backpack. He pulls out a small box. "It would have been harder to do this alone."

I frown. "What's that?"

He opens it carefully, revealing the contents. Letters. Pressed flowers. A lipstick print on a napkin. My heart stops when I see the handwriting on the back of an envelope. Mom's. "Time to move on, don't you think?"

"Daddy, why'd you bring all of Mom's stuff?"

"I'm going to bury it," he says and then snaps the lid shut. "Time to close the chapter."

I wait for him to explain further.

"Is that okay with you, Ames?"

"Why now?" I ask in a meek voice.

Dad sighs and looks out before him. We've managed to pick a pretty scenic view for a pitstop on our way to the peak. Burbank unfurls before us. Home.

"I got what I wished for. She came back. And it was all wrong. And here we are, a year later, and I think I'm finally ready to accept that all of that...what she did..." He grabs my hand. "It was so wrong, Amy."

I've never heard him talk about her like this. Without some level of sympathy.

"What she did to you girls, most of all. I already sat through your hurt once. Then she comes back and throws everything topsy turvy again. She's...not a good person."

That stings. After all, I'm half of her.

As if reading my mind, Dad continues. "Don't get me wrong, you girls got the best of her. The looks for one."

"*Dad...*"

He laughs. "I'm kidding. Well, not really, but you know that's not the most important stuff."

I blink. "You think she'll never come back?"

"I'm not the type of person to say never. But, how does that saying go? When people show you who they are, you have to believe them."

My heart wrenches up into my mouth as all the text messages I've sent my mom over the past year come into focus. I've always thought it had to do with me. If I say the right thing, let her know how much I miss her or love her, if I time it right, then I'll get that text message I want so badly.

Her actions are not and have never been a reflection of me.

They're about the coldness in her heart. That's her own problem.

"You okay, sweetheart?" Dad nudges me with his elbow.

"No," I reply and then smile.

He smiles back and leans his forehead to my temple. "You've been going through it. You want to talk about it?"

I shrug. "I just...don't feel like enough. For anyone."

"Oh, honey –"

"You don't count. You're my dad."

He holds himself back from saying the obligatory, "Not just because I'm your dad," thankfully.

"I can't get my publisher interested in any of my story ideas. Nothing I think of is 'light-hearted' enough. I'm barely sleeping. And whenever I'm not thinking about work I'm thinking about Hunter. And I hate it."

Dad tsks. "What for, Amy?"

"Because I've been with him like, what, two months? I shouldn't feel this enmeshed. This responsible for –"

"It's because you care for him. Nothing is wrong for you. You've always had such a magnanimous heart."

"Seriously? Magnanimous at a time like this?"

Dad scoffs. "You know what I mean. Big heart. You've always loved so easily. That makes it even easier to get a broken heart."

"Yeah, there's a reason I haven't dated. And this is it."

"Well, there's no reason to hold back your love just because you're afraid of being hurt. That's a silly way to live."

"It's a safe way to live."

"Well, *fuck* that."

I laugh. "Dad!"

"Seriously. Fuck that. I fell in love. I got hurt. But I also have five beautiful daughters, and if not getting hurt means I never got the five of you, well, that sounds even worse."

"You're such a sap."

"You love it."

He kisses the side of my head, sweat of his upper lip brushing my skin. I push him away, cringing with laughter. "Daddy, stop it!"

"Look, you and Hunter...this is a complication. But if you're willing to give space for it in your life, then that means it's a complication worth having."

I look down at the box of Mom's things. A life can only have so many complications at once without totally breaking down. Dad has invited me here to give me an opportunity to let go of one of them.

I think it's time.

I carefully take the box. "I'll carry this the rest of the way."

"If that's what you want, pumpkin. You ready?"

We climb the rest of the way to Verdugo Peak. Though the Solace family subscribes to the messaging of, "Leave only footprints, take only pictures," a moment like this calls for a little disruption.

Dad pulls out a small trowel and digs up a hole underneath some nearby brush. When it's deep enough, I hand him the box.

He places the box into the hole takes a breath and then stands up. A single tear rushes down his cheek, but he smiles despite it. "That feels good."

Watching Dad let go of Mom is all I need to let go of her too. I take his hand. The only parent I need, right here. The one who has never flinched away.

I want to be like him when I grow up.

In fact, with Hunter and Jessica, I can be that.

Fuck Veronica. Fuck all the complications. I'm showing up for what I love. Magnanimously. Fully.

With hope I haven't allowed myself to have in a long time.

24

HUNTER

When my assistant told me that there was someone asking for me at the front desk of the Ricks Corporation building, the last person I expected to walk through my door was Hank Turpin.

I shoot out of my chair to meet him. "Mr. Turpin, what a surprise. I wasn't expecting you."

Hank tries to greet me in return but has to take a moment to catch his breath. He's panting, clearly having run the whole way. "I have news," he wheezes, pulling a handkerchief out of his coat pocket and blotting his face.

I lead him to a chair and pour him a glass of water as he cools down from his sprint. He drinks the entire glass in one go, a drop of water dribbling down his chin.

"My god, man, what happened to you?"

Hank slams the glass down and then smiles at me. "I've got the double whammy for you."

I lean on the edge of my desk. "Lay it on me."

"Well...Your girl's new fiancé –"

"She's not my girl."

"It's an expression, Ricks. In my line of work we use a lot of expressions. Stay with me."

I resist a smile. Maybe the reason Hank is so out of breath is he had to climb out of the pulp detective novel he was written into.

"He's a drug dealer. A big one." He then pulls out a stack of photos from his jacket and lays them on the table.

I glance down at the mugshot of Greer Daniels. Except that's not the name on the board he holds below his sneer for the camera.

"Gary Dawson. I swear, these guys and their aliases. They're so lazy."

My heartbeat quickens. "Okay, so she's wrapped up with a drug dealer."

"No court is going to give custody to a woman wrapped up with a drug dealer. Especially the likes of Dawson. This guy's gone as far as plastic surgery in order to keep up his drug operation. Involved with the cartels. It's a whole thing."

I pale at the thought of Jessica having to even be near this freak. I know it's an impossibility now, but being a father, the what ifs are never far from my mind. "She's probably on drugs, then."

"She wouldn't be able to sneeze without ruining a pile of cocaine. You think a former addict can resist that?"

I gulp. "That's great news." That's the only time news like that has been described as "great".

Hank smiles. "Yes, the first whammy. But the second —" Hank pulls out an old timey tape recorder from his jacket pocket. Jeez, what year does this guy live in? "Just in case we get one of those sympathetic, millennial judges, I've got motive."

I frown. "Motive?"

He presses play on the recording. First, I hear Hank's voice. "I want to move ten kilos to a place with a more northern exposure, you catch my drift?"

I glance at the PI, a jolly smile on his face. "You posed as a –"

"Shhh, you'll miss it."

"Listen, our supply is down," Veronica's voice replies. From the quality of the sound on her end, it sounds like a phone call.

"Oh, don't give me that shit," Hank retorts.

"We don't have it," Veronica hisses. "But if you want to be in touch in October –"

"What the fuck is going down in October?"

Veronica hesitates. "Let's just say my business is going to be opening a new line of income. And our supply issues won't ever come up again. How does that sou –"

I shut off the recorder before I hear anymore. The room is silent as I piece it all together.

The hearing is at the end of the month. If Veronica gains custody, she not only gets her alimony, but she also gets child support for Jessica. Only someone as cold-hearted as Veronica would use custody of her child as a "new line of income".

I knew something was wrong. *I knew it.*

"That must have been hard to hear, Ricks. I'm sorry I didn't warn you."

I shake my head, although I feel like I'm going to be sick. "N-no, you...this is good."

"It is," he says encouragingly.

I take a deep breath and rub my forehead. "Fuck."

"I know this is all a lot to take in. But remember, this is good. It's a good thing."

I nod. "Yes. You're right."

"Everything we need is right here. And don't worry. I've backed it up to the cloud too."

I can't resist a chuckle. This older man's charm knows no bounds. "Thanks, Hank."

"Don't mention it. After all, with the rate you're paying me, you could say I have a new line of income coming in."

We both laugh. Takes the sting away from finding out how absolutely heartless Veronica is. Always has been. Somewhere inside me, I had hoped she had changed. If just the tiniest bit. Not for me. Not even for Jessica. But for her.

After all, I loved her. I saw her at deep points in her addiction where she couldn't function without coke. I was... I guess I was too immature to get her the help she needed at that time.

Why wouldn't she want to get better for her? For her *life?*

It doesn't matter. That's not my problem. This is sorted. Nearly done and dusted. Which means I can go back to how life was before Veronica showed up and bungled this all up.

I can go back to Amy. With a full, unafraid heart.

I can love her without the fear that my whole life will turn upside down and watch her feel responsible for turning it right side up.

Yes, I can love her. Because I do. I have for a while, but I'm now finally free to see my feelings for what they really are. Unafraid.

I need to let her know as soon as possible.

25
___

AMY

Even just walking into Ricks Melrose is hard to bear. Seeing his last name everywhere drives me crazy. It's not just the sign over the entrance. It's written on the walls, emblazoned on the cocktail napkins that I use to hold the tiny spoonful of tuna poke I swiped from a passing cater waiter. I can't even enjoy the view of Melrose from the rooftop, I'm so consumed with Hunter's name.

Axel and Gillian's engagement party isn't a huge affair, but every event with all the Solace sisters ends up being fairly large with all our plus ones. Axel, Gillian, and Stella are a threesome. Dana brought Drew (just kiss already!), Harley is obviously accompanied by Grant and Tana, which means Victoria also tagged along, and Kira even brought a friend from the office. She works so much I didn't even know she had friends. Then, of course, you have the Hitchins family, Jeremiah, Lola, and even Axel's father, Paul, with whom I've heard there is a lot of tension. Throw in a couple other friends here and there and this is a banger.

I obviously invited Hunter. Dad did too, I think. And he said he'd come. Although, I think he was just being polite.

It's nearly time for dinner service and there's been no sign of him.

"Please have some fun, Amy," Gillian scolds me. She's looking beautiful in a mint green gown, her long waves pinned into milkmaid braids.

"I'm having a great time, what are you talking about?" I shove the spoonful of poke into my mouth.

She purses her lips. "You're not good at hiding how you feel."

I swallow the tuna whole. "That's not true."

"Sure, that's why you're standing over here by your lonesome, all sad like your ice cream fell off the cone," Gillian says.

"Hey, that's not true, I'm talking to people, I –" I stop midway through my defense when I see Hunter walk through the archway of ivy and roses over the door onto the roof. He's alone. No Jessica. I watch him scan the party for me. And then his eyes catch mine. A smile creeps onto my lips.

Gillian follows my gaze and chuckles knowingly. "You've got it so bad for him."

"Shut up," I say, slapping her arm.

Hunter starts to walk toward us. My cheeks heat up.

"I'll make myself scarce," Gillian says, then kisses my cheek softly. "Love you."

"Love you too..." I reply nearly inaudibly, not bothering to watch her walk off. I can only watch Hunter as he comes closer and closer. It's like we're the only people in the entire world, two spotlights coming together until they collide.

He stops about a foot away from me. "Hi."

"Hi. You came."

"Of course I did. I said I would."

I beam.

"I know I should make my rounds first, but I want to talk to you first. Is that alright?"

I glance at the party. I can tell some of my family and friends are trying very purposefully *not* to look at us. "Yes. I'd like that."

Hunter smiles. His beard is freshly trimmed, hair swooped back into a slick bun. "There's a table over here..."

He holds his arm out for me. I wrap my hand around his bicep carefully, trying not to communicate my need through my touch, but I can't help it. When he's this close to me, I want to make sure I won't lose him.

Hunter guides me to a standing table near the edge of the roof. It has undoubtedly the best view of LA from here. Somehow, for being in the heart of LA, enmeshed in the din of a party, the world feels so quiet.

I lean nervously on the table and look out at the view. "Your place is stunning. Thank you for offering it for Axel and Gillian."

"What are friends for?"

I look at him for just a moment before it becomes too much for me to bear. He looks devastatingly handsome tonight.

"You look beautiful, by the way," Hunter says. *Dammit.* He beat me to the punch. "Is it alright if I say that?"

I nod. "Absolutely."

A grin spreads across his mouth. "Good. I like the daisies."

I touch the bodice of my daisy-printed dress and smile.

Hunter then clears his throat. "Well...I have news."

I hold my breath. *Please let it be good. Please let this all be a good sign.*

"I'm going to win the custody case. My PI found

indelible proof that Veronica is unfit to be a mother. There's no way I'll lose."

I gasp. "Oh, Hunter. That's wonderful. You must be so relieved!"

"I am," he says.

"I mean, I feel relieved, but you must – oh my gosh –"

"That isn't what I wanted to talk about, though."

My stomach drops again. The bad news could come at any second, like a slap to the face.

"I want to talk about us. What we are...what I think we could be."

I grow several inches when he says that, my chest filling up with hope.

"I don't come from love, Amy. I come from convenience and money," Hunter says. "I don't know if I ever really loved Veronica even. It just seemed like the next right thing to do. Especially if I wanted a family. Anyway..."

I don't know what to say, so I just look at him, trying to stay as present and open as possible.

"I've been scared I don't have room for you. In my heart. Not because you're too much or...it's because my father had the emptiest heart known to man. Every boy in some way aspires to be like their father. And while I detested the man most of my life, a part of me wanted *to want* to be like him. But he was callous. And..." Hunter stops and looks askance.

I reach out and touch his hand that rests on the small table. "Hunter, you can tell me anything. It doesn't scare me."

Liquid gold eyes flick into mine.

I squeeze his hand. "Really."

Hunter's usually intense eyes soften at the corners. A flick of a smile on his mouth. "I watched my father be cruel to my mother my entire life. I hated him for it. But it also made me not so great with women myself. My twenties were...a mess. I was fucking up left and right by everyone's standards. Couldn't hold down a girlfriend, slacked off at the office...I was such a disappointment to them after being the golden, only child, prepped to take over the family business one day."

He clears his throat and runs a hand through his hair. "I knew my dad wasn't a good man. But when I walked in on him fucking his secretary in the office, I lost it. I didn't hesitate to tell my mom. Finally, a reason bad enough to have her walk away." His eyes glaze over. "But she didn't. She just said that *that* was the way of our world. I was so mad at her. How could she accept that? Why wasn't she mad or running out the door never to return?" His eyes turn to me. "I get it now. She had her security. She had me. And...even if she shouldn't have, she loved my dad."

"That must have been really hard."

He nods. "So, I said that's not going to be me and I walked away. They cut me off, stopped talking to me."

"Oh my god, even your mom?"

Hunter keeps nodding. "Let's just say I can relate to you in that way."

My heart breaks for him. No. For us. Both of us have had all this love to give that people don't seem to want.

"Then, I met Veronica, fucked around, married her, was about to have the family I knew I could have without my parents involved and then –" He snaps his fingers. "They were gone. Plane crash."

I'd be lying if I said I hadn't read the articles. A tiny passenger plane going down in the middle of a storm on the Great Plains.

"So, I had to come back to all of this. Run the family business. I wouldn't have done that if Jessica wasn't on the way. And when Veronica left, I couldn't help but think I was just another version of my father. Cruel and –" He stops himself. "That's why I haven't pursued relationships until now. Has seemed safer not to get attached. Not just for me. For everyone. I'm afraid that there's just some inherited nature in me that makes me like him. And I –"

"Stop that. You're not that at all. *At all.*"

Hunter smiles meekly. "Thank you."

"Seriously. You have a heart. A big one, Hunter."

He stiffens his jaw to keep from getting emotional. "I'm glad you think so."

I caress his hand softly. "I probably didn't make it any easier to overcome that every time I've brought up your past or –"

"It's only reasonable for you to worry."

"I'm not worried. Not anymore." I look him dead in the eye. "It was never about *you.* It's always been about me and –" *Just tell him. He's the one you want. There shouldn't be any secrets.* "It might sound crazy, but the gate was about a lot more than just you. I figured it out in therapy and realized that…I used to see Malcolm sneak out through the gate. I was young and didn't know, but –"

"Oh, Amy, I'm so sorry," Hunter says emphatically. "You were so young, you –"

I pinch back tears from my eyes. "It's okay. I'm glad I know now. Because that's unbuckled so much of that strange tension from how I felt about you. It never had to do with you at all. You're wonderful."

He flushes. I can see it through his beard. "I don't know about that."

"You are, Hunter. You are." I look at our hands positioned so yearningly together. "I deleted my mom's number."

Hunter doesn't say a word, just widens his eyes in shock.

"It's time for me to move on from people who don't love me the way I need to be loved; don't you think?" I ask gently. "Maybe both of us...maybe we deserve this. Us."

Hunter's lips spread into a smile. He touches my chin, tilting my face up toward him. "I have to agree."

When he kisses me, it's like I've never been kissed before. His lips are both tender and straightforward, a shovel breaking into fresh earth. I pull myself into his arms, run my hands up his chest. Finally, things feel settled.

"Hey you two! Get a room!" Axel shouts. "It's our engagement, not yours!"

I hold up my middle finger toward the party, relishing the burst of laughter after it. "Don't you dare stop kissing me," I say in the space between a kiss.

"Trust me, I'd kiss you forever if I could," Hunter answers, pressing a hand against my lower back with possession.

I can't wait to tell him he *can* if that's what he wants. I'd be happy to give him my forever.

Both our brains are addled with champagne by the time we return to Hunter's house. He lets the babysitter go after exchanging a few words about how the night went with Jessica. Thankfully, Jess is sound asleep and didn't cause any trouble whatsoever, except she did require five books to be read to her before she'd lay her head on the pillow.

A girl after my own heart.

The second Hunter closes the door behind the babysitter, he pulls me into his arms and kisses me with the intensity of the noonday sun when the sky is clear. It is hot, passionate, and I need more, more, more.

We don't make it upstairs this time. Instead, we dance back and forth between kisses into the kitchen, giggling at how easy it all feels.

"Great party," Hunter mumbles halfway through a kiss, shucking off his sportscoat.

"Yes, I'd have to agree," I reply. In turn, I undo the top few buttons of my dress.

"Ah-ah-ah, that's my job," Hunter intercedes, his hands knocking mine away casually. As he undoes each button, he kisses and laps at my neck, lower and lower until he reaches the swell of my breast. "My favorite part."

I giggle. "That's your favorite?"

"Well, let me be clear. They're all my favorite," he murmurs. "I like these..." He cups my breasts. "I like *these.*" Grabs my ass, pulling my hips to his. "But most of all..." Hunter gazes down into my eyes. "I like this."

I bite my lip coquettishly. "What?"

"Your beautiful face. Perfect lips, brilliant brown eyes, your nose."

"My nose?!"

"Oh, come on, that's a normal thing to like."

I narrow my eyes. "Is it?"

"Are you trying to tell me you *hate* my nose?"

I consider his nose for a moment. Strong, aquiline. "No, I love it."

"Yeah, you better. Considering what it can do when I –" Hunter grips me under my arms and lifts me onto the counter.

I hold in a quiet squeal as he pushes the fabric of my dress back, rips off my underwear, and dives between my thighs, lips and tongue (and nose) working and nuzzling eagerly.

Relief spills into my belly, heightening the pleasure as he laps and sucks. I stretch my arms out over the counter and let out a pleased sigh. "One day, I'm going to have to have you in my mouth."

Hunter stops suddenly and lifts his head, eyebrows cocked. "Listen, I'm in no rush, but the second you want to, you let me know." He leans over me, resting his elbow on the counter next to my waist while his thumb idly encircles my clit. "Literally *the second* you know, I'll come running." He pushes a finger inside me, pumping it delicately. "I will come running."

I try to steady my breath, but the way he's got me gripped outside and in makes it a struggle. "E-even if you're at work?"

"Oh, god, if you called me in the middle of the day, begging for my cock, I would combust right then and there."

I laugh but am cut off when a ding of pleasure rocks my body. "I-I'll wait, then. Would h-haaaate for you to combust before I – I – I – "

Hunter removes his hand just before I can hit the crest of pleasure. "Wait right there for me, baby."

I stare up at the light fixture over the kitchen island that barely hovers on, the bulbs burning low like candles. *Stay...I* encourage that rolling boil in my belly. *Please stay.*

The zing of Hunter's zipper interrupts my concentration. I feel the head of his cock pressed up against my pussy. "Oh, Amy..."

I clutch his hand to my hip as he enters me with control and poise, not eager for it to be over despite his excitement.

Hunter touches my face with his other hand, guiding

my gaze into his. He wears an encouraging smile. "God, you're the most beautiful –"

"*Stop that,*" I say in jest. I never want him to stop that.

"No, you can't make me," he replies as he begins to roll his hips.

I'm so distracted, I don't even realize how he's entered me unsheathed and how easy it feels to have him enter me so fast. Thankfully, I have prepared for this. A quick visit to the gyno a couple weeks ago yielded me a prescription for birth control so I have less to worry about. *Less.* Not nothing.

Still, though...it feels so much better when he's bare inside me.

"Beautiful Amy...most beautiful girl – *woman* – in the entire fucking world," Hunter murmurs, bestowing sloppy kisses to my neck.

I adjust my face to catch his mouth with mine, lock my legs around his hips, and moan. Those actions encourage him to go faster and faster.

Hunter suddenly stands upright and tucks his hands against my thighs. This gives him all the leverage and control he could possibly need to take us to the very end.

"Oh, Hunter," I moan, my voice squeaking as I try to control the volume. I fumble around to grip his forearm. "Go, go, go."

He's working so hard he can't speak. All he manages are affirmative pants and breaths.

"Look at me," I say. "See me."

The second our eyes lock, my body bursts with heat and fire. My back rises off the cool marble countertop and I stifle a wail in my hand. Hunter gasps, bending at his waist as if he's just had the wind knocked out of him trying to catch a football. His hands loop around my wrists as he falls forward. I feel the rush of him inside, warm and wet.

His eyes look to mine with fear, but I shake my head. "It's okay, it's okay. It's safe."

Hunter's eyes flutter shut. He presses his forehead to my bare clavicle. I can feel his breaths against my chest. I cradle him there. Mine. My man.

My love.

"I love you," I say raggedly. It's not an accident. "Hunter, I –"

He lifts his head and kisses me fiercely, unfathomable for how much energy we've just spent. When the kiss breaks, he retreats only an inch so he can speak as clear as day: "I love *you*, Amy Solace."

I loop my arms around him, hugging him close, my chest filled to the brim with love for him.

This is why we had to let go of our pasts. To make way for the love we both deserve. This one, right here, Hunter and me.

Love that feels like you're flying and even if you fall, the earth will be there to welcome you back with tenderness.

26

HUNTER

Veronica looks nice sitting directly across from me at Sam Serty's conference table. Almost like she's not a fucking drug addict. She's gotten better at hiding it, although that might just be the Dior saddle bag and splash of Chanel No. 5.

Her lawyer, a woman in a burgundy pantsuit with a piece of jewelry shaped like a beetle on her collar, as severe as they come, organizes some papers in front of her and then smiles humorlessly. "Well, shall we?"

In the case of a custody trial there is, of course, the trial. But there is also the *pretrial hearing. And* there's the meeting *before* the pretrial, which Sam refers to as a "four-way meeting" between the parties and their respective attorneys to try and narrow the issues that will be admissible to be brought before the judge.

Little does Veronica know, we're not getting that far.

Sam was lovely enough to host at his office. This is where we're going to stage our coup. We met up an hour beforehand, girlishly giggling at the gotcha moment we've organized with the help of Hank's information.

"Well, I don't think this will be very long," Sam says with a sigh.

Veronica's attorney raises an eyebrow. "Oh."

Sam and I exchange a look before Sam opens the audio file of the phone call on his laptop. "Please let me know if you remember this phone call, Ms. Ricks."

I bristle at the fact she still uses my last name.

Veronica can be as cool as a cucumber, but I see fear flashing on her face. *What phone call?*

Sam presses play. Hearing the conversation breaks my heart all over again. And watching her face fall makes it even worse. However, once it's finished, Veronica immediately snaps, "That was recorded without my consent."

Sam grins. "Ah, so you remember…"

Veronica huffs. "In California, you need two-party consent to –"

"We're happy to take that case on if that's what you'd like to file. However, given the information contained in this recording, I can't imagine courts would be too sympathetic to your plight," Sam says.

Veronica's attorney's face is hardened as a rock. I can't get a read on her. Is she shocked? Embarrassed? "Well, you probably can assume we don't want that used at the trial."

"Sure, which is why – um, Harold?! Can you come in here?!" Sam shouts through the door of the office.

The man, Harold, enters, holding a clear cup.

"This is my friend Harold. He'd be happy to administer a drug test for you, which, in turn, would –"

"I won't do it," Veronica answers.

Her attorney reaches out in front of her. "Relax."

"I won't. They have no reason to believe I'm –"

"We have every reason to believe you're using, Veronica," I growl.

Sam clicks his pen. He explained that's his way of letting his clients know to rein it in rather than bringing attention to it aloud. I purse my lips tight together so I don't say anything else out of turn.

"She's my daughter. I have a right to –"

"Your client, D'Angelo," Sam says to the red-suited attorney.

"*I have a right!*" Veronica yells and then turns to her lawyer. "You said I have a –"

"You do," D'Angelo says coolly. "At least, you did. But this…"

Veronica collapses into her chair, wide green eyes crawling into mine with desperation. "Why don't you want me to have a relationship with her?"

I don't speak. I'd like to laugh. The fact she's still putting on this ruse after it's been made obvious what she wants is…well, it's embarrassing for all of us.

"Let's recalibrate, hm?" D'Angelo murmurs to Veronica.

"Sam, this would be a good time for those documents we were talking about," I say to Sam.

"*What* documents?" Veronica sneers.

I shake my head. "How do you expect to get anything you want with that tone, Veronica?"

Sam clears his throat and pushes the documents over to D'Angelo. "As you can see, we're requesting that Ms. Ricks waive her parental rights as well as her last name."

D'Angelo leans over to examine the papers in front of her. Veronica's eyes stare so hard at me I'm afraid she might drill holes through my skull.

She doesn't scare me, though. I have the power here.

"What do we get out of this?"

"Well, this information was found out by a private investigator. We know we're both in the business of justice, but in the interest of my client, we'd be happy to sweep this little hiccup under the rug and allow your client's continued...business endeavors," Sam explains.

I hate that *that's* the deal we have to strike. However, Sam has assured me that there's no way they can legally hold us to that. When the time comes, we'll let the proper authorities know.

D'Angelo clearly takes no guff. Maybe I can get her on my legal team when we aren't on opposite sides of the table. "That's quite an allegation, Mr. Serty, I –"

"I'll do it. I'll sign."

We all look at Veronica. She said it in a voice that was barely audible and yet we all heard it.

She's giving up. I'm sad to say I knew she would.

"We're so glad you're amenable to that, Ms. Ricks."

"Please stop calling me that," she replies, face empty of expression.

"That's your name, isn't it?" I growl.

Sam clicks his pen.

D'Angelo tries to lean over to whisper something to Veronica, but my ex-wife just waves her off. "Give me a fucking pen. It will be worth it so that I never have to be called that name again."

As soon as she gets her hand on D'Angelo's beautiful Mont Blanc, she slams the pen onto the paper, ferociously scribbling off her initials and signatures wherever required.

"I didn't realize you'd break so easily," I mutter. "You sure you care about your daughter or –"

"Bite me, Hunter," Veronica spits through grit teeth.

"*Your client*, D'Angelo."

D'Angelo scoffs. "You think I can control her?"

I resist laughing along with her.

"There, are we done?" Veronica shoves herself up from

the table and doesn't wait for a response before she storms out of the conference room.

D'Angelo sighs and stands. "Pleasure doing business with you gentlemen."

"Likewise as always, D'Angelo."

The attorney struts out of the room, dropping the document in front of me. "Congratulations, I guess."

I stare in silence at Veronica's messy signatures, touching the paper ever so gently, afraid it might evaporate into a million pieces if I'm not careful.

"She's mine," I whisper.

Sam claps a hand on my shoulder. "All yours."

I'm not a touchy man. I'm a professional after all. However, I throw my arms around Sam, squeezing him tight. "Thank you, thank you, thank you."

Sam bear-hugs me back. "It's moments like these that remind me how much I love what I do. You're welcome, son."

I might not have had a father who loved me the way I want it. But the way the men in my life have shown up for me through this – Kent, Sam, Hank – make me realize how worthy I am of the love he couldn't give.

My heart is so full.

"Now that all ties are finally cut, go out there and get 'er, huh?" Sam encourages, patting me on the back and out of the office.

I immediately clap eyes on Jessica who is sitting bewilderedly in Amy's lap. The two of them must have seen Veronica storm off. I hope she didn't say anything stupid to upset my daughter.

My daughter.

I barely make it a few steps before I fall to my knees and open my arms wide. "Jess –"

She leaps out of Amy's lap and runs into my arms, giving me a big hug. The first hug in months where I haven't been scared to lose her to Veronica. I can't hold back the torrent of tears. They spill into her dark hair.

"Daddy, are you crying?" Jessica asks worriedly.

"I can't help it, I'm sorry."

She smiles, cupping my cheeks in her tiny hands. "It's okay. Even daddies need to cry."

I chuckle, though the tears keep rolling down. "Happy tears, baby. They're happy tears."

Over Jessica's head, I see Sam briefing Amy on what has just happened. Her hand is clutched to her chest, a breathless smile on her face. When she turns to look at me, the picture completes.

I lift Jess into my arms as Amy comes toward us, then close the gap, wrapping my free arm around Amy's back and kissing her softly. "She's ours," I whisper.

"I know. I heard."

"You're my mommy now, Amy? I mean – Mommy?" Jessica asks, her eyes flicking between both our faces.

I hesitate to answer, trying to read Amy's expression. Jessica might be fully mine now in terms of the law. But really, she's ours. Mine and Amy's.

"That's up to your daddy, I think," Amy says, softly rubbing Jessica's arm.

"If you're comfortable with it, I...I don't see why not," I reply.

Our eyes lock. Less than a week ago, we were up in the air. Now, we are making a life together, deciding we are a real family, right here. It might be too quick by some standards. But for us, it all feels just right.

Amy smiles and then pinches Jessica's chin familiarly. "Then 'mommy' it is."

"Yay! Daddy *and* Mommy!" Jessica jovially shouts.

My heart is overflowing. She's never been able to say that in her whole life. "What do you say we get some ice cream?"

"Mm. Only if there's chocolate," Jessica says.

Amy laughs. "Jess, there's always chocolate."

Jess grins. "That's what Daddy always says."

I put Jessica on the ground between us. She reaches up for both our hands and together, the three of us walk out of Sam Serty's office as a family. And as we go down the street, I revel in the first time feeling of getting to show off my daughter with the person I love.

The person who chose us.

27

—

AMY

TWO MONTHS LATER...

IF SOMEONE WOULD HAVE TOLD ME A YEAR AGO HOW much my life would have changed in seemingly the blink of an eye, I wouldn't have believed them. However, it's truly amazing how beautiful your life can become when you give into it and let the universe take you where you need to go.

In fact, letting my mom go and solidifying things with Hunter (and Jessica) was exactly what I needed to get my writing back on track.

Only a week after Hunter received full custody and full parental rights to Jessica, I was standing in a meeting with Kris, Fiona, and the editorial interns, pitching an idea for my next book.

This was the one that stuck.

"Oh, Kitty, I knew you could do it," Kris replied after I finished my presentation, clapping her hands together, starry-eyed and smiling. "You've pinned it just right, I think."

I had smiled gratefully to Fiona. Though she can be caught as the middleman between editor and writer, she didn't give up on me for a second. When the idea came to me for what is my latest book, I called her quite literally in the middle of the night and she stayed up for hours with me, trying to work it out.

You're Priceless, Petunia was fast-tracked for production and publication.

I got my hands on the advanced reader copies this morning, and *of course*, the first people who get to see them are my family.

All my sisters and my dad are piled into the room for the occasion, as is our tradition. Everyone is reading studiously to themselves, even Stella who can now read picture books entirely on her own. Her reaction has been the cutest to watch because of how, from time to time, she'll laugh or gasp at something.

I'm watching my dad most of all. He cries after every single one. And it's clear as he turns page after page, he's getting choked up.

I can't blame him. This book is probably the closest to my heart. Yes, even more than the one about divorce.

This one is about *me*.

In it, everything seems to be going right for Petunia. Her dad packs her favorite lunch, she is team captain in kickball, she gets invited to a party. But nothing *feels* right. Nothing feels good. And it's all because Petunia doesn't love herself enough to recognize love in others.

"Brilliant!" is how Kris had described the idea. "You found the meeting of the complicated and the simple. This is just –" My posh British editor had actually squealed.

Kira finishes first. A speed reader to her core. As soon as she closes it, she smiles at me warmly. Kira's never been one who needs to say much with her words. Her face always says it all.

You did good, sis.

"Oh my god," Gillian says as she closes the book. "Seriously, Ames?"

I grin and shrug.

Dana and Harley finish up soon after that. And then Dad, who has to take off his reading glasses to wipe his eyes free of tears. "Oh, Daddy…" Dana goes over to his armchair and squeezes in next to him.

Her comfort just makes him cry harder. And then she's crying.

"You guys, you can't –" I look back at Harley, the one with the stiffest upper lip, whose lower lip is trembling. "Harley!"

"We can't help it! It's – it's beautiful," she says in their defense.

Stella looks up, frowning. "Everyone, shhh! I'm not done."

While Stella continues to read the book carefully, word by word, we all crowd around Dad's chair. He wraps his arm around me and kisses the side of my head. "Well done, Amy. That was the best one."

"You say that every time," I whisper.

"Because it's always true! They just get better. Although this one might be my favorite."

It goes without saying to everyone that the Petunia books are somewhat autobiographical. Stories, anecdotes, personality traits…there's a little or a lot of me emblazoned in every story. So, I think it's obvious to everyone that this one is about me through and through. No one needs to call it out. All they need to do is see it.

Gillian rubs my shoulder and Harley plops down at Dad's feet, resting her head against his knee.

"You all are getting too big for this," Dad mutters.

"*Getting* too big?" Dana scoffs. "We've *been* too big for a long while now, Dad! Won't stop us, though."

We all let out a loud laugh and immediately shut up when Stella glares at us.

Finally, Stella slams the book closed and exclaims, "Wowwowwow! Aunt Amy! That was good!"

"You sound surprised!" I reply, thankfully getting it all out before she bounds over to me and gives me a big hug, knocking the wind out of me.

"We always love you, Amy," Gillian says.

"Yes, it goes without saying, however..." Kira says, turning her chin up thoughtfully as she leans on the back of Dad's chair. "We could all afford to say it more."

I smile at her. "To everyone."

"Yes, definitely," Dana says. "Let's make a pact."

We all agree and then collapse onto Dad's lap from our various places on the easy chair. When we were little, we all would have given him our full weight until he jokingly, breathlessly would cry out, "Uncle! Uncle!" Now, however, we have to be a bit more controlled about it.

"Oh, my girls! Where has the time gone?" he remarks, hugging us all toward him, including Stella who is just the right size to burrow into his lap.

"Someone's phone is buzzing," Harley announces.

"Mine!" I cry out. "Let me go everybody, let me –"

We disentangle with some amount of effort. Dad's not the only one getting older, after all. Once I get out of the mess and hop onto my feet, I check my phone. Text from –

"*Hunterrr...*" Gillian teases, looking over my shoulder.

My sisters all erupt in a chorus of "oooh" before Dad shushes them. "You're adults!" Stella continues despite the joke having ended; she's at that age.

"You know, adult doesn't mean anything! Not really," Harley says, tapping Dad on the shoulder.

I start to open the text but feel overwhelmed by everyone watching me. "Why are you staring at me?"

"Yeah, why are we staring at her?" Stella echoes.

"We're not staring," Kira says, quite obviously staring.

"Yeah, not at all," Dana adds, doing a better job than Kira of lying.

I shake my head and turn around, finally opening the text.

Meet me at the gate? :)

I resist swooning, especially with twelve eyeballs glued to me. This has become a habit of Hunter's. Inviting me out to meet him at the gate. Sort of demystifying it as a point of trauma in my memory. Associating it with something much better. *Him.*

The past two months of our relationship have been... more incredible than I could have imagined. The second we let go of all the things holding us back was the second we were able to fall into each other completely. I can barely remember my life before him. We've almost completely woven our lives together, a braid decorated with wildflowers of a life. I still live at home. Don't want to give my dad a heart attack by moving *too* fast. Between the way Harley and Gillian have gone about things over the past year and change, I feel like he deserves a break.

And don't even get me started on Jess. She is truly the light of my life. Every time she calls me "Mommy" I alight with glee. Now, children can be difficult, this is a given. However, I adore her even when she's difficult. I want to make her life better. Want to give her another shoulder to lean on, another heart to call hers.

With a partner like Hunter at my side, it's easy.

"I'll be back in a few minutes. Just got to go see what he wants," I say, rolling my eyes, feigning being put out by his request.

"Oh, don't make that face," Harley comes up to me and slaps my butt playfully.

"Hey!" I laugh as I skip out of the living room, through the kitchen, and into the yard, a big smile on my face. I stop suddenly. "Shoot, I forgot –" I turn around and nearly smack into Kira who is holding a copy of my book. For Jessica. I take the book and press it to my chest. "Thanks, sis."

She shrugs. "Seemed important."

I nod and then continue on my trajectory across the yard.

Closer and closer to the gate. It doesn't hum with the same sense of dread it once did. It makes my heart beat faster in a good way, puts butterflies in my stomach I love to feel, makes me think about my future with Hunter and Jessica.

My family.

I grab the gate latch, twist it open, and throw open the gate with a smile. "I have a surprise for –"

I stop speaking immediately when I see Hunter kneeling on one knee before me. Ring box in his hand. Jessica at his hip, beaming ear to ear.

The book falls from my hands, I'm so shocked. "Wha... what..." I can't even formulate a coherent sentence. I shut my eyes for a second and shake my head as if that will reset the world. Clearly, this is an alternate reality.

When I blink my eyes back open, though, the image hasn't changed.

"Amy, you alright?" Hunter asks, half-smiling nervously.

"N-never better," I say.

Hunter is dressed up, white button down and a purple bowtie which matches Jessica's dress perfectly. They're a perfect little duo.

"So, I think you know what this means..." he says with a smile.

I nod, putting my hands over my mouth in shock.

"I want to keep it short and sweet. I love you. *Adore* you. I want to marry you."

"And I want you to be my mommy, but like *really* be my mommy," Jessica chirps.

I grin so hard my cheeks hurt and tears spill out of my eyes.

"Will you marry my daddy?"

I shake my head in disbelief, though my answer is an adamant, fervent, "Yes. Without question."

Hunter doesn't have a chance to put the ring onto my finger before I fall to the ground and take them both in my arms, bestowing kisses to their cheeks over and over.

My family. My adorable little family.

Here and now, I promise, I'll never hold back my love again. Without letting it all go, I never would have found the two greatest loves of my life.

Continue to read Dana and Drew's Story Faux Beau's Baby Surprise